"We never see each other," Francesca declared

"You always have excellent reasons for breaking dates, for not being home—but what it amounts to is that I live in the country and you live in London."

Oliver's frown was deep, his gray eyes hard. "So you turned to Matt for company, is that what you're saying?"

"I'm not having an affair with Matt—leave him out of this."

"How can I do that, for heaven's sake? I always knew Matt fancied you, but I never thought he'd make a play for you behind my back."

"Matt hasn't done anything. When you didn't show up last weekend, I decided I had to get away. I want a life of my own. I want to live in London, and I want a job as interesting and absorbing as yours!"

CHARLOTTE LAMB began to write "because it was one job I could do without having to leave the children." Now writing is her profession. She has had more than forty Harlequin novels published since 1978. "I love to write," she explains, "and it comes very easily to me." She and her family live in a beautiful old home on the Isle of Man, between England and Ireland. Charlotte spends eight hours a day working at her typewriter—and enjoys every minute of it.

Books by Charlotte Lamb

Don't miss any of our special offers. Write to us at the following address for information on our newest releases.

Harlequin Reader Service
901 Fuhrmann Blvd., P.O. Box 1397, Buffalo, NY 14240
Canadian address: P.O. Box 603,
Fort Erie, Ont. L2A 5X3

CHARLOTTE LAMB

runaway wife

Harlequin Books

TORONTO • NEW YORK • LONDON
AMSTERDAM • PARIS • SYDNEY • HAMBURG
STOCKHOLM • ATHENS • TOKYO • MILAN

Harlequin Presents first edition August 1990
ISBN 0-373-11290-4

Original hardcover edition published in 1989
by Mills & Boon Limited

CHAPTER ONE

FRANCESCA stepped back from the dining-table and surveyed it from a little distance, smiling at the sheen of highly polished silver, the scallops of lace on the cloth, the crystal bowl of dark red roses in the centre.

'Looks really romantic, doesn't it?' Mrs Hine said beside her, cramming her apron into her carrier bag as she spoke.

'Yes, doesn't it?' agreed Francesca, her dark blue eyes switching to the other woman's face. 'Thank you for staying on so late to help me get everything ready.'

'That's all right, dear. It was a pleasure; I hope you have a lovely evening. That duck smells delicious already; I've left the cherries on the side to be reheated in the microwave, and the oranges in Grand Marnier are in the fridge. I think that's everything...ooh, I nearly forgot...' Mrs Hine rummaged in her bag again and pulled out a large envelope. 'Happy Anniversary, Mrs Ransom.'

'Oh...thank you...you're so kind.' Francesca pulled out the big, glossy card and smiled, very touched. Mrs Hine observed her expression with satisfaction.

'I'm glad you like it. Now, sure you wouldn't like me to stay and serve the dinner, and wash up afterwards? You don't want to be rushing in and out on a special night like this...'

Francesca laughed softly, mischief in her eyes. 'Mrs Hine, when we were first married I couldn't afford to have anyone to cook or clean for me. I did it all myself, and enjoyed doing it. Thanks for offering to stay, I appreciate all the help you give me, but tonight I'd like to have my husband all to myself. I won't even bother about the washing-up tonight, it can be done tomorrow.'

Mrs Hine winked. 'I get you. Mr Ransom's always that busy, isn't he? Be a special treat to have him all to yourself for once. Well, enjoy yourselves.'

She bustled out, the front door banged to behind her, and when she had gone Francesca carefully placed the card among the handful already standing on the white marble mantelpiece above the fireplace.

Few people had sent them anniversary cards, few people knew it was their anniversary, and she was quite content with that because the cards which had come were all from people she loved and knew loved her. She did not want an avalanche of cards, like those which came each Christmas, from business connections of Oliver; customers or suppliers, people who worked for him or bought from him, or had met him socially, or wanted to—all the hordes of London acquaintances her husband seemed to have. Oliver apparently knew hundreds of people, most of whom Francesca had never met. His secretary usually dealt with the straightforward business cards sent to his London office, but there were still a great many who wanted to claim a more personal relationship and sent their cards to his country house, to be opened and gazed at blankly by his wife. Each year there seemed to be more of them, and they increasingly took some of the meaning out of Christmas, for her.

There was no anniversary card from Oliver himself, but he had sent her the dark red roses she had arranged so happily on the dinner-table, her hand tender because, although she often received bouquets of flowers from her husband, for once she could be absolutely certain it had been Oliver himself who had chosen these, not his secretary, the super-efficient Miss Sylvester. Only Oliver knew that the first flowers he had ever sent her were dark red roses, which had cost far more than he could afford at the time. She had scolded him, tears of pleasure in her eyes, because they needed every penny of his salary for more essential things than roses, but he had kissed her and said, 'One day I'll send you so many red roses you'll be smothered by them.'

Eyes fixed in memory, she stared at the mantelpiece without seeing it for a moment, then suddenly focused on the Victorian clock standing between the cards and gave a cry of horror at the time. Oliver would be home any minute and she wasn't dressed yet! She flew up the stairs, unbuttoning her blouse as she went, turned on the shower as she shed the rest of her clothes, then carefully fitted a shower cap over her blonde hair and stepped under the lukewarm jets of water. She had timed this whole operation perfectly, and now she was running late and would have to hurry over this very important part of the evening. Damn!

She stiffened as the phone began to ring. Now, who was that? She had intended to set the automatic answering machine; she must do that as soon as the phone stopped ringing. Thank heavens Oliver wasn't home yet. It would almost certainly be for him—at weekends calls were mostly for him—and she did not want anything to distract him from her tonight. Stepping out of the shower, she took off the plastic cap, shook her long hair free, wrapped herself in a loose, white towelling robe, ignoring the insistent ringing until it stopped, and then rushed downstairs and switched on the answering machine. Any further calls would be re-routed and could be dealt with tomorrow.

She went back upstairs into her bedroom and gently towelled herself, putting on the white silk lingerie she had earlier laid out on the bed; a lace-trimmed bra, a lacy teddy, suspender belt, matching slip, ultra-fine stockings. She was quite tall: a slightly built girl with pronounced cheekbones, large, deep-set blue eyes, a wide, finely cut mouth. Viewing herself before she slipped into her dress, she sighed over her lack of curves. She was too thin, her breasts small, if rather nicely shaped; she lacked the sort of sex appeal she would love to have.

People always said blondes were sexy, but they didn't mean her type of blonde. Her hair was so pale it was almost silver; she wore it long because Oliver had often said he preferred it that way. For years now she had wound it on top of her head in an immaculate chignon because Oliver said it made her look elegant, and if she couldn't look sexy she could at least look elegant for him. The reflection she was staring at was too familiar; she had been looking like this for so long, she couldn't remember the last time she had made any changes to the way she looked, and it had been Oliver's preferences which dictated her appearance, although it had been an age since he had paid her any compliments, or indeed made any comment on how she looked.

Was that what was wrong with their marriage? The lack of surprise? Maybe she should have her hair cut in a new style? Buy totally different clothes, change her image? She turned her head this way and that, imagining herself with short hair, in vivid, flamboyant clothes... then laughed and picked up her white silk dress to step into it.

This, too, was elegant, a classic design which clothed her slender body in Grecian folds and suited her hairstyle to perfection. Oliver hadn't actually picked it out, but she had done so with his taste in mind, knowing he would approve.

Now she wryly considered it. Well, it wouldn't set the world on fire or make men gasp with desire at the sight of her, but it was very suitable for the wife of a very wealthy and important businessman. Was that how she wanted Oliver to see her tonight, though? She put her head to one side, grimacing.

Maybe she should take off the dress and just wear the undies? They were sexier, at least! She pictured Oliver's expression if she opened the door looking like that!

'Happy tenth anniversary, darling,' she could say, putting her arms round his neck. On their very first anniversary, actually, he had found her in the bedroom getting dressed, taken one look at her in see-through black undies, and had swept her off her feet and carried her over to the bed. They had never bothered with dinner in the end, just snacked at midnight on cold chicken and salad, but Francesca knew that was very unlikely to happen tonight. The fire in their relationship had gone out long ago. Well, ten years is a long time, she thought, then looked at her watch, frowning.

Oliver should be here; perhaps traffic leaving London had been heavier than usual? He was driving himself home. In town he usually had a chauffeur, since parking was such a problem, and it saved time for someone else to drive, drop him somewhere and come back for him when required, but when he came home he always drove his cherished vintage Jaguar, now fifty years old but kept in perfect condition with loving care.

She sat down at the dressing-table, applied foundation, dusted powder over it, added a little blusher, painted her lids with mauve eyeshadow, brushed her lips with coral pink, then assessed herself again before adding some jewellery: a gold torque around her neck, a matching bracelet for one wrist, small gold stud ear-rings. Well, she looked rather more striking now! She sprayed herself generously with Oliver's favourite French perfume, which he always brought her back whenever he went abroad, and hurried back downstairs.

She paused in the panelled hall to listen for the unmistakable note of the car, but only heard the rustle of wind among the sycamores in the garden until the phone rang, making her jump. It cut out as the machine came into operation and she relaxed again.

Where could he be? He had said he would be home by seven, and it was a quarter past. The smell of the roasting duck was more pronounced; she had better go and check on it before it burnt.

She went through into the kitchen, put on an all-enveloping apron to protect her dress, and slipped on oven gloves. The duck was coming along fine; she put it back into the oven but adjusted the temperature downwards as Oliver hadn't got here yet. Duck was her son's favourite, too; she always cooked it for Jon on his birthday, but he liked it stuffed with oranges and served with orange sauce. Oliver preferred cherries. On the table stood the vegetables which she would put on to cook as soon as her husband arrived; French beans, carrots, mange-tout.

Mange-tout was another of Jon's favourites. She missed her son badly; her days had revolved around him since his birth. She had been perfectly happy and busy down here in Sussex while Oliver was away abroad, or working in London, because Jon needed her, and both she and Oliver wanted a tranquil country life for their only child. This was a beautiful old house; Jon loved it as much as she did, had had a happy childhood, and she didn't regret for an instant deciding not to live in London. But now that Jon was away at boarding-school she was in-

creasingly lonely. She had always known that Oliver
meant Jon to go away to school when he was eight,
and she usually accepted all her husband's decisions without argument, but over Jon going away
she had fought him.

Oliver had been surprised; almost incredulous.
he was a very important man now. He employed
hundreds of people who all jumped when he said
jump. People didn't argue with him—least of all
his own wife! When Francesca said she did not want
Jon to go away Oliver had stared, his black brows
jerking together, his grey eyes cold with impatient
disbelief. He was a very tall man, with an incisive,
angular face; but it was his personality which was
most dominating, and Francesca had had to
summon all her courage to challenge him.

'You know I've had Jon's name down there since
he was a year old. Don't be ridiculous. He'll soon
settle down. Other boys do, why shouldn't he?
Unless you've been putting silly ideas into his head
and telling him he won't like it there?' His narrowed eyes had stabbed at her and she had felt like
running away.

'Of course I haven't!' she had protested nervously, yet had stood her ground in the face of
Oliver's displeasure, which probably surprised him
even more. 'I haven't said a word to him, but he's
so small, too young to go away from home yet.
Can't it wait another year?'

'Eight is when all the other boys start there.'
Oliver's mouth had been hard with insistence.
'Jon's quite mature, he'll cope. Don't try to make
a baby out of him.'

That word had silenced her, pain had flared in her dark blue eyes and she had bent her long, slim neck, her throat closing in anguish. Oliver had won because she couldn't bear to say another syllable, although she doubted if Oliver realiscd why she suddenly capitulated. She was sure he would not knowingly have hurt her. He had used that word without thinking.

Jon had gone off to boarding-school looking very small and helpless to her, leaving this house cold and empty, and herself without an occupation. She had had a few scrappy notes from him since; it sounded as if he was gradually getting used to being away from home, but even if that eased her mind a little she was still lonely.

She had never been able to have another baby after Jon arrived. She had hoped for years, she had even had tests at a fertility clinic, but there seemed to be nothing wrong with her; the doctors couldn't explain why she had got pregnant with Jon within weeks of beginning to try for a baby, yet now seemed unable to do it again.

Oliver had never been as eager for another child as she was; he had been happy enough just having his son. He'd felt Francesca should stop worrying about getting pregnant again and concentrate on Jon. They had plenty of time, he said; they could think about another baby once Jon was older. But as the years passed and he became more and more successful, and more and more busy, he and Francesca saw less and less of cach other, and that second baby remained a shadowy dream for her.

If she had had other children, especially if she had had a daughter, she wouldn't be feeling so low, because someone would still need her, but, as it was, she had decided that she must do something to change the pattern of her life. She must either have another baby or get a job. Life couldn't go on the way it had lately, or she would go crazy.

The phone began to jangle again; after the third ring the answering machine took over. Francesca took off her apron and went slowly to the window to look down the drive to the high iron gates. They were electronically controlled and had been made by one of Oliver's own companies. When he arrived he would operate the remote control in his car, and the gates would swing open for him.

Turning, Francesca stared at the phone, biting her lip. Oliver was now nearly half an hour late. That would not surprise her any other evening, but he had promised faithfully not to be late tonight. He knew she was cooking a special meal, timed exactly for eight o'clock, and this was their tenth wedding anniversary, for heaven's sake! It wasn't any other day of the year!

But what if something had gone wrong? What if these telephone calls were from Oliver explaining that he would be late? He could have had an accident, he could have broken down on the way home. Anything could have happened.

She leaned over to rewind the machine, then played the messages recorded on the tape, her body taut as she recognised the woman's voice.

'Mrs Ransom, I'm so sorry...' Miss Sylvester had a voice dripping with charm; it matched her luscious appearance. She was a redhead with feline green eyes and the smile of a cat that had stolen someone else's cream. 'Mr Ransom has been called to an emergency board meeting. There has been a serious incident in the Welsh factory. He asked me to apologise and say he would be home as soon as humanly possible, but not to wait dinner for him.'

Francesca sat down on the nearest chair and dropped her head into her hands while the other woman's sweet voice murmured on.

'Such a pity... your anniversary, isn't it? I hope you liked the roses. I'll be in touch as soon as there's news.'

The second call was from her father-in-law. 'Fran? I just heard on the news that one of Oliver's factories has blown up. Let me know if there's anything I can do. I'll be at home all evening.'

She lifted her head, her eyes dark with tears, trying to smile. Typical of Harry, to have heard so quickly and to guess what it could mean. He didn't say so, but he was offering to come round and keep her company while Oliver hared off to Wales. Harry knew how much she had been looking forward to this anniversary weekend; he knew how hard it would hit her when she was cheated of it.

The third call was from the local newspaper, trying to get hold of Oliver. She got up and reset the machine before the Press rang again; they would mostly be ringing his London number, especially the national papers, and Oliver had Press relations officers to deal with them, but Francesca did not want to talk to anyone who thought of ringing here.

She went to the window again and watched a harvest moon climbing through the dark sky. She wouldn't see Oliver this weekend. He would be off to Wales; perhaps he was already on his way there. She had a fatalistic sense of hopelessness.

It had been her first real chance for ages to get him to herself, talk to him, make him see how she felt—and now it would pass and things would go on as before. Oliver would be as busy as ever. He would drive down some weekends, but usually he would bring guests, important people he wanted to impress, clients he wanted to charm, foreign visitors who were dying to see the picture-book England this house represented for some people.

She sat on the deep window-seat, staring into the cream-walled drawing-room with its English chintz at the windows and covering the deep, comfortable chairs and sofa. A restful room, with a traditional English Axminster carpet on the floor. All around hung watercolours Francesca herself had painted: views of the garden, the old, timbered house, black and white, the red roof crooked with age, framed in its trees, the river swirling just below, and in the distance the smooth turf of the green and white downs running to the sea a mile beyond here.

She had spent many summer days happily painting on that riverbank while Jon fished or swam in the river, or lay on the grass beside her, reading a book. She remembered her tranquillity then with melancholy. Things would never be the same again.

* * *

When she played back the tape of telephone messages next morning after a lonely breakfast, she discovered that Oliver had, indeed, gone to Wales. Miss Sylvester smoothly conveyed his apologies again and said he would be in touch himself—as soon as he could find the time to ring! Francesca sat and watched autumn leaves blowing along the garden paths. Soon it would be winter. She felt cold already.

She couldn't stay here a minute longer. She had to get away and think. She picked up the phone and rang the London office. Miss Sylvester could give Oliver a message from her, for a change.

Miss Sylvester wasn't there. She was in Wales with Mr Ransom, Francesca was informed.

She slowly put the phone down and stood up, shivering. It was getting colder by the minute. It was nine o'clock. At ten Mrs Hine would arrive and ask questions Francesca did not feel up to answering.

She ran upstairs and opened her wardrobe, pulled out a few things, packed a case without really thinking very much about what she was taking, put on a sheepskin-lined suede coat and went out through the kitchen to the garage where her car was parked, pausing en route long enough to write Mrs Hine a short note explaining that she was going away for a few days. Just as she drove out of the garage she saw Mrs Hine unlocking the side door in the stone garden wall. Francesca didn't stop or even slow down. She drove on, gave Mrs Hine a wave and shot out through the gates which closed automatically behind her, aware of the older woman staring after her, eyes wide. No doubt news of the explosion in Wales had reached the village. The local grapevine worked efficiently. They might even know Oliver hadn't come home last night.

Well, now they would have something else to talk about. When Oliver finally did ring, Mrs Hine could tell him Francesca had gone away. How would he react to that? Or perhaps he wouldn't. Maybe he would just shrug and go back to the more important subject of his company. Miss Sylvester would soothingly advise him not to worry, no doubt. Miss Sylvester certainly wouldn't be worrying. Oliver had once said that he often talked over problems with his secretary; she might be stunning to look at, but she also had a mind like a man, tough and incisive, he had said in admiration.

Francesca wished she had someone to talk over problems with, someone she could trust the way Oliver trusted Miss Sylvester. If her parents were still alive she could go to them, but her mother had died six years ago, and her father had followed within a year. Francesca missed them, especially at this moment. She had loved her parents and often wished Jon had known them. He barely remembered his grandfather, and did not remember his grandmother at all.

Francesca had no brothers or sisters, either. Her family hadn't been a close one; she had an uncle in Scotland whom she never saw, and an aunt in New Zealand, who occasionally remembered to send a Christmas card—but apart from that her only family was Jon and Oliver.

She could go to Harry, of course, but, fond though she was of him, he was Oliver's father and she couldn't talk frankly to him this time. It wouldn't be fair to Harry. He thought the sun shone out of Oliver.

Where was she to go? Come to that, she thought wryly, where was she going? She had merely driven without thinking, on automatic pilot, and as she looked about she saw that she was now on the main London road and heading towards the capital.

Well, why not London? It was a big place, easy to get lost in London, and she needed to get lost for a while. She had to think, and although the country was a quiet place it was harder to be alone there. People were too friendly. If you were alone they came up and tried to get into conversation. They noticed things, asked questions, tried to find out who you were and what you were doing there, miles from anywhere. London was very different. You could drop dead in the street in London and people would politely step over you and pretend there was nothing odd about lying there on the pavement getting colder and stiffer by the minute.

She reached the city just before noon and checked into a charming if small hotel in a back street behind Oxford Street, in the very centre of the West End. She had picked it at random while she was driving around because it had an underground garage right next door where she could park her car overnight. At tremendous cost, of course, but at least it would be safe.

Her room was furnished in Laura Ashley style and was very comfortable. She unpacked, making a face over the odd things she had packed. Well, she could always buy anything else she needed. Oliver was very generous; she had an ample bank balance and several credit cards. Money wasn't one of her problems.

That afternoon she walked around London, window-shopping and exploring the central area. She didn't know London well; she was a country girl who came from Romney Marsh in Kent, which was where she had met Oliver, shortly after her eighteenth birthday. She had been working in a village library while she waited to go to art college later that autumn. Oliver had been visiting his father in Rye and had dropped in to her library to look up some local history. He had asked her out for lunch and three months later, instead of going to art college, she had married him.

It had been that fast, that overwhelming, for both of them. She knew Oliver hadn't intended to marry so soon—he had been older than her, but he hadn't yet begun to make the sort of money his company was later to make. He had needed every penny he could scrape together; he had even persuaded his father to mortgage his house, and Harry must have half expected to lose that money. He hadn't, of course. He had long ago been repaid and now held valuable shares in the company, but ten years ago the company had existed only in two minds, those of Oliver and his partner, Matt Keilner.

Matt was the inventive genius behind it all; he created the electronic gadgetry Oliver marketed with such flair and success. They had been at school together and were close friends, which was surprising in itself, because Matt was very much a backroom boffin, the loner type who rarely emerged from his workroom and was scared stiff of other people. Francesca only knew him vaguely.

Occasionally, over the years, Oliver had winkled Matt out of his shell and dragged him home to lunch or dinner, quite often at first in their poky little two-room flat in Maidstone during the first year of their marriage, when money was so tight, and then to each of their homes in turn as the company grew and prospered and they moved up-market until they ended up at Lambourne five years ago.

Success had come quite fast. Electronics was a business which moved at the speed of light, and Matt was a brilliant man, shy and inarticulate, clumsy and uncertain in human relations, but blindingly clever. Francesca felt quite at home with him when she did meet him, because she didn't need to feel that Matt expected anything more of her than she had to offer. She was shy, so was he; she didn't find it easy to make small talk, nor did he. They sat in silence together and listened to music; it had amused Oliver.

'You two are a matching pair!' he'd teased them at first, then as time went by he was rarely at home himself for long and he stopped bringing Matt. The two men still worked closely, and the company was still dependent on them both—on Matt's inventions and Oliver's business capacity.

Francesca stood still on the pavement, thinking. People swerved round her, exclaimed irritably, 'Do you mind?' or 'Excuse me!' She hardly heard them as she processed an idea. Suddenly she swung towards the road and hailed a passing taxi.

The company headquarters had recently moved into a modern office block in the eastern edge of the City of London. Francesca had only been there twice: the day Oliver signed the lease and took her and Matt out to lunch to celebrate—and one day when she and Jon were shown around the two floors which the company occupied. Oliver had invited them, but he had been detained on urgent business and it had been Matt who showed them around. He was never as shy with Jon. Children weren't as alarming to him, perhaps. He had taken them out to lunch in a fast-food place; he and Jon had vied with each other to eat the most beefburgers and drink the most milkshakes. Jon had had a great time, and Francesca had enjoyed the day, too. She always liked to see her son looking that happy. Matt was a nice man. Jon thought so. She did, too.

That afternoon, Matt had told them quite a lot about himself in one way or another, she remembered, looking at her watch eagerly. He had mentioned casually that most days he went for a walk to clear his head at around four o'clock in the afternoon, and stopped off for a burger and a milkshake before going back to his workroom. He might have made that up for Jon's benefit, but on the other hand he might have told the truth.

It was a quarter to four when her taxi deposited her outside the office block. She walked to and fro on the pavement, watching the main entrance, now and then looking at her watch as time ticked past without any sign of Matt. The uniformed commissionaire noticed her and came over to the great plate-glass door to stare out at her. Francesca halted in front of a shop opposite and stared into the window with her back to the road. She could still see the office block reflected in the glass. The commissionaire walked away. She saw him salute casually as a jogging figure went past him and emerged into the street.

It was Matt; a very tall man in a green and cream track suit and green track shoes, his brown hair ruffled and untidy, his body loping easily in practised strides. Francesca ran after him, calling his name, and he slowed and turned to stare, then stopped dead.

'Francesca?' His brown eyes were wide with surprise. She saw a scar on the side of his cheek and remembered him telling Jon that it was inflicted years ago by a very bad-tempered pet monkey. Matt loved animals, even when they were unpredictable.

She caught up with him, smiled shakily, nodding. 'Hello, Matt.'

He stared down at her, pushing his windblown hair back from his face and frowning. 'Are you looking for Oliver? He isn't here, he's in——'

'Wales. I know. I was waiting for you, not Oliver.'

'For me?' His voice was comically incredulous, and she laughed more in affection than amusement. Matt was really rather endearing. She liked that shyness of his; he was more human than Oliver. He was more her sort of person; she and Matt were both less able to face life than Oliver had always been.

'Yes, for you,' she said. 'I need to talk to you, Matt. I need your help.'

'Is something wrong?' Concern shaped his puzzled gaze. 'Is it Jon? He isn't ill? Has there been an accident? I know where to get in touch with Oliver in an emergency—come back inside, up to my office...'

She shook her head as he tried to pull her back towards the office block. 'No, it isn't Jon, it's nothing like that. I just need to talk to you, Matt. Can we go somewhere quiet where we won't be interrupted?'

'My office?'

'No. Didn't you tell Jon that you had a beef-burger somewhere around here every afternoon?'

He looked startled. 'Did I? You do have a good memory. It's true; there's a little place half a mile from here. I always jog there and back and stop half-way for a hamburger and milkshake. I never eat lunch unless Oliver drags me off with him; it breaks up the day too much. I like to work through the day until mid-afternoon, then have an hour off, and when I get back I'm fit for another four or five hours' work before I go home.'

'I've been walking around for hours, Matt. I'm dead tired. Could you skip your jog today, and just walk at my pace to this fast-food joint? Would you mind? You can jog back after we've talked.'

'OK,' he said, and they set off side by side. She felt Matt eyeing her sideways, waiting for her to start talking, but somehow it was much harder than she had imagined it would be when the idea first came to her. It had seemed simple, then. Now she had cold feet.

'Bad business, this explosion in Wales,' Matt said after a silence. 'Oliver doesn't know yet whether it was carelessness or an inherent design fault in the equipment. If it's the latter, we're in trouble.'

'It must be very worrying,' she said, only then looking at the events of the past twenty-four hours from Oliver's point of view. She had been so busy concentrating on her own problems and fears that she hadn't thought about what was happening to Oliver. 'Nobody was killed, though, were they?'

'Two people were injured. Thank heavens, it was a lot less serious than we'd feared at first, but any problems with the electronic equipment can be potentially disastrous for us. Bad publicity for us.'

'That's why Oliver had to go to Wales at once,' she accepted flatly.

'Exactly.' They slowed in sight of the restaurant, which was almost empty. Matt gave her a boyish grin. 'I'm starving. I never think I'm hungry until I get here, then my stomach starts clamouring for food. A Pavlovian reaction, I'm afraid. How about you? Eaten today?'

'Yes, but I'll have a cup of coffee with you.'

'Fine. You sit down at a table while I get the food. Want a doughnut or a hot apple turnover?'

'No, thank you.' She picked a table in a quiet corner and sat down. A moment later, Matt joined her, carrying a tray of food; french fries, hamburgers, strawberry milkshake, coffee. He sat down and handed Francesca the coffee, then began eating hungrily. She stirred cream into her coffee and waited for a moment to let him sate his hunger a little. No wonder he was so thin, his face angular and bony. He obviously didn't eat a proper diet.

She told him so a little scoldingly and Matt grimaced at her.

'Don't you start. Oliver's always nagging me about my diet. That isn't what you needed to talk about, is it? Oliver didn't send you to nag me into eating at regular hours?'

'No,' she said huskily.

He finished one hamburger and carefully wiped his fingers on a paper napkin, then looked up at her thoughtfully. 'What is wrong, Fran? I know something is, I can see it in your face. You're pale and you look far from happy.' He looked down again, cleared his throat, still automatically wiping his fingers, although they were quite clean now. 'If I can help, just ask, you know I'd do anything for you,' he muttered in a low voice, and she was very touched.

'Thank you, Matt.' She kept her eyes lowered. 'I do need your help. I want you to get me a job.'

'A job?' He looked totally astounded, staring at her.

'With the company,' she added, and Matt took an audible breath.

'I don't understand,' he said, after a long pause. 'Why ask me? Why haven't you asked Oliver?'

She looked up again and their eyes met. Matt frowned. 'Or have you? Did he refuse, is that it? Fran, I'm sorry, but I can't interfere between you and Oliver, you must realise I can't.'

'I haven't even breathed a word to Oliver,' she said. 'I know how loyal you are, Matt, and how long you and Oliver have been good friends.'

'Since we were ten years old,' he said, as if she didn't know all about it.

'I know, and I know that's why you wouldn't tell me if he was having an affair with anyone.' She watched Matt's face intently and saw the shock in it, the redness rising under his skin.

He didn't answer that time, just stared back at her, his mouth tightening. His silence was as good as a reply, and Francesca's eyes filled with the anguish she felt. She looked away, blinking to stop the escape of the tears which were burning under her lids. Matt would hate it if she cried. He hated this already; he was stiff with embarrassment and misery.

'I'm not going to ask you anything like that, Matt,' she said, letting him off the hook. 'But will you give me a job? I can't stand it down in Sussex by myself a minute longer. I'll go crazy. I miss Jon so badly, and the house runs like clockwork. I'm not needed there any more, except in the holidays when Jon's home. If I could have another baby it might be different, but I can't, and I'm bored and miserable. I got married too young, I think. I missed a lot and I'd like to catch up on things. Work in London, have a flat up here, meet people——'

'What about Oliver?' Matt burst out, looking distraught.

'Oliver?' Francesca looked through the window at the busy street. Her dark blue eyes were remote now; she had forced all visible signs of pain back below the surface, hidden them away. 'I've left Oliver,' she said quietly. 'And I am not going back to him.'

CHAPTER TWO

SHE spent the following day going around London looking for an unfurnished flat, and finally found one in a Victorian house in Finchley, a northern suburb close to the wooded heathland of Hampstead. The flat had two rooms: a small bedroom with a cubicle of a bathroom leading off it, and a sitting-room which housed a minute kitchen/dining-room area on one side of it. After the spacious elegance of Lambourne the flat seemed tiny to her, but she had lived in smaller places in the past, she knew she would get used to living here.

There was an antique shop on the corner of the street. Passing it on her way back to her hotel, Francesca spotted a Victorian chaise-longue in the window and pulled up on impulse. She parked and went back to the shop just as the owner was getting ready to close. He was amiable enough to stay open a while longer while Francesca inspected the red velvet-covered chaise-longue. She bought it and several other items which she felt matched it: a Victorian oak sideboard and a round table of the same golden wood and the same period, and a faded and rather threadbare Persian rug.

'Will you deliver these tomorrow?' she asked as she handed him her credit card, and the shop-keeper looked doubtful, scratching his head.

'Depends where you live.'

'Ten doors down from here,' Francesca said, smiling.

'Oh, in that case, sure.' He took her signed voucher and grinned back at her. 'Morning or afternoon?'

'Late afternoon? Around four or five? I've got a lot to do tomorrow.'

On her way out she noticed a basket chair, but decided she had bought enough furniture for the sitting-room. The less she had in that room, the more spacious it would seem.

'You can have that at half-price,' the shopkeeper said. 'It's a Lloyd Loom chair with the original cushions in it.' He smilingly watched the struggle in her face, murmured, 'It's a bargain at that price,' and saw her weaken.

'I'll write you a cheque for it,' she said in wry defeat.

'You can pay me when I deliver the stuff tomorrow,' he said, waving her out of the shop and locking up after her.

She had an appointment with the personnel department next morning. Matt had fixed it; Matt was surprisingly efficient when he put his mind to something. Francesca was going to be using her maiden name, and she gave as her address the flat in Finchley. Matt had obviously ordered the personnel manager not to be too inquisitive. She knew Francesca was Oliver's wife but that fact was never mentioned; indeed, the woman gave no sign of curiosity, nor did she stare or seem particularly interested. Francesca gave her full marks for discretion and professional ability.

'We'll want three references,' Miss Dilney said, handing her a printed form to fill in. 'Standard practice, I'm afraid. We need to be sure we're taking on someone trustworthy.'

Francesca gave three references: Matt, her father-in-law, her solicitor in Sussex. She listened carefully as Miss Dilney explained the contract she would be asked to sign, and also such matters as tax and national insurance stoppages from her monthly pay cheque, all of which came as novelties to Francesca.

Life was rather more complicated than she had realised. She had jumped into this without thinking it out, or having any idea what it would entail, but she was becoming hourly more sure she was doing the right thing.

She might have gone on for years down in Sussex, drifting further and further away from Oliver without knowing what was happening to them. She would have been desperately lonely and unhappy, and heaven knew what the final outcome would have been. Divorce? Yes, probably.

She could have talked to Oliver, but what good would that have done? He wasn't going to change the way he lived and worked; he was obsessed with building this company. He would have soothed her, perhaps, or been irritated with her for making such a fuss. He would have jumped to the conclusion that she was angry because he hadn't turned up for their tenth anniversary; he would impatiently have explained why he had had to go to Wales. Even if she had said that she understood that, and that it hadn't been the root cause of her decision, merely the trigger which made her realise that her marriage was virtually over, Oliver wouldn't have believed her or taken what she said seriously.

He hadn't taken her seriously for years; she had merged with the wallpaper of his life, along with Lambourne, Jon, even his father. The things that really mattered to Oliver were up here, in London. This was where Oliver lived. Their home in Sussex was a place he visited, and she and Jon people he visited; they were peripheral to Oliver's real world, the business world in which Miss Sylvester and Matt belonged and where Oliver most truly existed, was most himself, a self Francesca did not know.

She had been living in a fool's paradise, remembering the man she had married ten years ago, loving him blindly, and blissfully believing that he was still the Oliver Ransom of today. He wasn't; her Oliver had gone for good, she had come to see that at last, and that was why she was here in London, why she had left Oliver. She couldn't live with that phoney marriage a day longer.

She had lunch with Matt; not in a fast-food place this time but in a very good French restaurant, near Covent Garden. Matt was actually wearing a dark lounge suit and his brown hair had been styled and was well-brushed and glossy, but he still looked uneasy in a smart striped shirt and silk tie. He kept fiddling with the tie and shifting in his seat, hardly able to meet her eyes.

'You look very elegant today, Matt,' Francesca said, with a smile at his discomfort. Matt was really very sweet, and she was determined to be cheerful today. She had spent enough time brooding; she was going through with her plans and she meant to enjoy herself. 'Is the suit in my honour?' she asked him teasingly. 'I'm flattered.'

He almost spilled his lobster bisque in his embarrassment, and Francesca patted his hand across the table.

'I just want to say thank you, Matt. I really appreciate everything you've done for me. You were the only person I could think of to ask for help—isn't that a confession? My one real friend, and I have to share him with my husband! I hope I won't have caused any trouble between you and Oliver, anyway. Put all the blame on me; don't quarrel with him over me, Matt, will you?'

He looked gloomily at her. 'I'll try not to.' He did not sound very optimistic about the prospect.

'Have you heard from him today?' She wondered if Oliver knew yet that she was not at Lambourne—or had he been too busy to ring her? She had left the telephone switched on to the answering machine. Miss Sylvester might have left any number of her honeyed messages and, unless Mrs Hine switched off the machine or answered it when it rang, Oliver might not yet know she had left home.

Matt nodded. 'We talked for half an hour early this morning.'

'He's still in Wales, though?'

Matt nodded. 'He's terrifically busy, Fran, sorting out what happened and what has to be done now. He asked me to talk to you if I had time, make sure you're OK.'

'You didn't tell him I was in London?'

Matt shook his head. 'You did say you didn't want him to know yet.'

'Yes.' She smiled gratefully at him. 'Thank you.' Then, looking down at her plate, 'And he has no idea I'm not at home?'

Matt grimaced. 'I doubt it, or he would have been different. He just said he hadn't been able to get you on the phone and there wasn't time to keep trying, could I ring you for him. He mostly talked about the explosion. It's a very disturbing business, you see, Fran. Oliver is sick with worry, try to understand . . .'

'I do,' she said, sighing, as the waiter proffered a mixture of fresh vegetables. 'Don't these look delicious? Do you come here often, Matt? I haven't been to Covent Garden for years and I hardly recognised the place; it's charming, isn't it?'

Her sudden change of mood had thrown Matt at first, until he realised she was acting for the waiter's benefit. He muttered something about liking Covent Garden's atmosphere and shops, and Francesca agreed.

'Oh, yes, I can't wait to wander around and take a look at some of the boutiques. I have some heavy shopping to do over the next couple of days, to furnish my flat. I bought some antiques—they're being delivered this evening—but I still need masses of things, from electric bulbs to tea towels. I'm not bringing anything up here from Lambourne. I'm going to buy my own stuff. I only hope I can persuade the shopkeeper who's delivering the antiques to help me arrange them the way I want them. He seemed quite obliging, so I may have struck lucky.'

'So long as he doesn't think he has!' said Matt, frowning. 'Maybe I'd better be there when he delivers this stuff? Seeing that you've got a man in the background will scare him off if he does have any ideas about you being a woman on her own. London isn't the country, you know, Fran. You're going to have to be careful. I don't want to scare you, but a woman living alone can be a target. You have got a chain on the door of this flat, I hope? If not, I'll fit one for you tonight. In fact, I'll look the place over and suggest some security measures.'

'You're very thoughtful,' Francesca said wryly, wishing he hadn't said any of that, because she was going to feel nervous when she had moved to her new flat and was alone at night. The dangers of life in London for a woman on her own hadn't occurred to her until now. 'Thank you, Matt, you're a darling,' she said, though, because she knew he meant well. 'And if you do have the time, please come—I'll even provide supper, of a sort. It will have to be a scratch meal, I'm not ready to give a full-scale dinner party yet. But I could do a spaghetti with a simple tomato sauce, or sandwiches and coffee... Which do you prefer?'

'Sandwiches would be fine,' Matt said, and she laughed and made a mock-furious face at him across the table.

'I see—you don't trust my cooking!'

He looked aghast. 'Oh, no, I didn't mean... I've always enjoyed your cooking, but I don't want to put you to any trouble. Why don't I bring the sandwiches? I know a great delicatessen near the office. I'll pick up some of their sandwiches on my way.'

'You won't. This is my treat. Anything you really hate, or shall I just make a selection and hope you like something?'

'I eat anything,' Matt said.

'Except my spaghetti?' she teased.

'I can see you'll never forgive me for that!'

Matt hurried back to the office after their lunch and she wandered around the narrow streets surrounding Covent Garden's old market hall; she found several bargains, which meant that she did not take the tube or the bus to Finchley, as she had planned, but hailed a taxi, which cost far more but was far easier.

She would have to watch the pennies in future, though. Taxis would be few and far between. She meant to live on what she earned; she wouldn't take money from Oliver. From now on she was going to be independent, learn to stand on her own two feet, which meant strict economy, and oddly enough she was quite excited by the thought. When they were first married they had had to think twice before they spent money, and that had been fun, especially as she and Oliver were sharing everything both at work and at home. In those days everything had been fun, come to that. She had been rapturously happy, and she was sure Oliver had been, too.

While she waited for her new furniture she put on her old jeans and a well-washed blue sweater and scrubbed out the flat; that reminded her of earlier years, too, when she had to do all her own housework. As soon as they could afford it, Oliver had insisted that she must have help in the house.

He had wanted her to have a nanny for Jon, too, but she had fought him over that. She loved looking after her baby, for one thing, and for another it was really her only occupation by then. Oliver wouldn't let her go on working for the company, and he wouldn't let her do the housework either. No wonder she had made Jon her full-time work!

She worked in a hurry, to be ready by the time the furniture arrived, and was soon flushed and a little grubby, her hair escaping from its usual immaculate chignon, long blonde tendrils curling down her hot cheeks. But for once it didn't bother her how she looked. Matt wouldn't even notice— he never really seemed to see anything much, he was so absorbed in his own thoughts; and it didn't matter what the man from the antique shop thought.

The doorbell went and she ran to answer it, wiping her wet hands on a towel, expecting the shopkeeper, although it wasn't yet quite four o'clock, then smiled in surprise at the sight of Matt. 'Oh, hello, Matt, you're early! I thought you were the man with the furniture. Come in.'

But he didn't move, just stood transfixed, staring as if he didn't believe his eyes, and Francesca realised she had been wrong in supposing he wouldn't notice the way she looked. She smiled an apology at him.

'Sorry if I look a sight, but I've been doing some cleaning. Would you like a cup of tea? I would, I've just finished and was thinking of putting the kettle on. I can't ask you to sit down until the furniture arrives, but at least the stove is working.'

'You look fine,' he said gruffly, looking down while his hand came from behind his back and was thrust out at her. It held a large bunch of amber-coloured chrysanthemums, their scent over-powering and melancholy with their familiar, unforgettable reminders of autumn smoke and falling leaves.

'Oh, thank you. How thoughtful you are, Matt. Flowers do make a place feel more like home, don't they? And I love chrysanthemums, especially this colour!' She lifted the great golden flowers to her face and inhaled their scent, sighing with involuntary nostalgia. 'Gorgeous smell, too. I'll put them in water right away. I haven't got a vase yet, but I bought an earthenware milk jug this afternoon in Covent Garden which will be the perfect home for these.' She grinned at Matt as she led the way into the flat. 'We'll have to have our milk out of the carton!'

Matt followed her into the sitting-room and stared around, his face appalled, while she was filling the green jug with water and arranging the flowers in it. 'Fran! This is worse than I expected. You can't live here! There isn't room to swing a cat.'

'I haven't got a cat, and if I had I wouldn't swing it. It sounds a cruel thing to do.' She smiled over her shoulder at him. 'Don't the flowers look great in this jug?' She placed it on the windowsill where the dying sun lit the sky behind the great, glowing blooms. Matt and Francesca stared, then she turned away. 'Well, how about that tea? Do you mind having it in a mug? I'm still in the process of getting my home together, and one of the things I bought in Covent Garden today was a mug tree with six mugs on it. I thought I'd make do with mugs instead of cups and saucers for the moment. I also bought six second-hand earthenware plates in a junk shop. They let me have half a dozen for five pounds, practically gave them to me because several of them had hairline cracks, but they're terribly pretty, and I was delighted to get them.' She was talking too fast and too much, because this was a tremendous step she had taken and she was feeling nervous, even though she was sure she was doing the right thing.

'I don't like this, Fran,' Matt burst out. 'You don't belong in a place like this. Lambourne is the right setting for you, that's where you belong.'

An angry flush crept up her face, her dark blue eyes flashing at him. She had been feeling unsure of herself a second ago; now her resolve stiffened and her chin went up. 'I'm a human being, not an object. I belong to myself, and I no longer want to live at Lambourne, any more than I want to live with Oliver.'

'Look, Fran,' Matt said jerkily, 'I realise it's none of my business...'

'No, it isn't!' she snapped. 'This is my life, not yours, Matt—so please don't say anything else.'

He looked even more unhappy. 'I have to! Oliver's my oldest friend and I care very much about you, too, Francesca. I can't help thinking you're making a terrible mistake, leaving Oliver. You won't be happy being alone, living in town; you're a country girl, that's how I always picture you—in the garden at Lambourne, among the flowers. On a hot summer's day when I'm working and the city's humid and sticky, I've often thought of you cutting roses and wandering across those marvellous lawns in a big straw hat with a trug over your arm. I don't suppose I've seen you gardening more than a couple of times, but it stuck in my mind, that picture of you, and I'd hate to think of you living in a little box of a London flat.'

Francesca's eyes opened wide in astonishment. That outburst was so unlike Matt! She couldn't believe he had really said it, and, from his flush and lowered eyes, neither could Matt! But he was still talking huskily, even if he wasn't looking at her.

'The city would be all wrong for you. You're just not used to this sort of life; you'll be miserable living alone in this poky little flat.'

The doorbell rang again and she hurried to answer it, grateful for the interruption. This time it was the man delivering her furniture. Matt helped him carry the chaise-longue, sideboard and table up the stairs to the second-floor flat, then the shopkeeper went back alone for the basket chair. When he returned he presented Francesca with a rather dusty amber glass Tiffany lamp with a brass stand which he had carried up in the seat of the chair. She was surprised and delighted; the lamp was charming and perfectly matched the other things she had chosen.

'It would be valuable if it hadn't been broken and mended rather badly,' he told her cheerfully. 'As it is, I'll throw it in with the rest.' He looked around the flat. 'The furniture already looks as if it belongs together! I hope you'll be very happy in your new home. Pop in again some time. I'm always getting new stock, and I'll be happy to keep my eyes open for anything that fits in with all this.'

When he had gone, she slipped into the bedroom to change, and then set out a meal on the oak table. She hadn't made sandwiches. She had bought a stick of French bread and some Brie and Camembert, which she served with a bottle of white French wine. Matt seemed to enjoy it.

'I must say, I like your idea of bread and cheese!' he grinned, sinking back into the basket chair, his long legs stretched out. 'Oliver must be crazy, risking losing you——' He broke off, grimacing, as the hot colour rose in her face. 'Sorry,' he muttered.

'Don't be silly, it was a nice compliment,' she said. They had been steering clear of any mention of Oliver, and Matt had embarrassed himself as much as her. 'Tell me more about this job,' she suggested, to change the subject.

'Oh, well, Oliver——' He stopped again, pulling a face. 'I can't talk about anything without mentioning his name, can I?'

'He's important to both of us,' she drily agreed. She could guess what he had been going to say. Oliver had often complained that Matt was stubborn about having secretarial help. He was intensely secretive and afraid anyone who knew too much would sell his latest innovation to a rival company. When necessary, Matt borrowed a secretary from someone.

It was because Francesca knew Matt's views that she had contacted him and asked him for a job. She knew there was one there, if she could only persuade Matt to let her do it, and she was sure Matt would trust her. He had known her almost as long as Oliver had; he knew she wouldn't sell the firm's secrets to anyone. Her only worry had been whether Matt would believe she could do the job.

'Thanks to Jon, I know my way around the company's computers,' she murmured. 'His room is crammed with the company's latest products, and I picked up the bug from him over the years.'

'I'm not really sure what you'll be doing,' confessed Matt. 'Except that you can take a lot of the routine, like paperwork, off my hands. I've never had a secretary of my own before.'

'We'll invent the job together,' she said, curling up on the chaise-longue and stretching with a yawn. She was tired. It had been a long day.

Matt was watching her with a smile. 'You look very elegant on that!'

'It was meant for more elegant times,' she said, aware that she was losing even more of the pins from her chignon, her blonde hair half tumbling down her back. She couldn't be bothered to tidy her hair again tonight; in a moment they would be leaving the flat. Matt had promised to give her a lift back to her hotel on his way home. 'Do you want another cup of coffee?' she asked politely, but he shook his head and got up.

'I'll help you wash these things up before we go.'

The doorbell rang and Matt stared at her, his brows together. 'Expecting someone else?'

She shook her head, puzzled. 'Maybe it's a neighbour, wanting to borrow a cup of sugar?'

'Or the friendly furniture salesman hoping to find you alone!' Matt scowled, making for the front door. 'If it is, I'll soon see him off!' He pulled the door open, his brows heavy, then he stumbled back into the room, while Francesca watched in startled surprise for an instant until she realised who had arrived.

Icy grey eyes were taking in the way she looked, still lying on the velvet chaise-longue, her blonde hair loose around her face, the softly flowing caftan creating an intimate atmosphere which was under-lined by the remains of their French supper, the two red candles, the empty winebottle, Matt's jacket flung casually on a chair, his tie undone, his shirt collar open.

'They say the husband is always the last one to know,' Oliver bit out between almost clenched teeth, and Matt looked horrified, went pale and then dark red, gabbling protests.

'You've got it wrong, Oliver, it isn't what you think, we were just going, I mean, nothing whatever happened, I was only helping Fran move in...'

'Don't lie to me, you bastard!' Oliver snarled, and leapt at him. Matt didn't even have time to get out of the way. Oliver hit him before he knew what was coming and Matt crashed backwards and sat down on the floor in a corner, shaking his head and looking dazed.

'Stop it!' Francesca was on her feet, trembling and trying to hide her fear as she faced Oliver. 'Leave him alone! He was telling the truth. We aren't lovers, we're just friends...'

'Do you think I'm so stupid I'll believe a lie like that?' sneered Oliver, his eyes contemptuous.

He took a step towards her and her breath caught with alarm, but she shakily answered, 'It's the truth! Matt had been helping me move into my new flat...'

'Your new flat!' snapped Oliver, looking around him, his black brows crooked with distaste. 'And who is paying the rent, I wonder? The same guy who was helping you move in, by any chance?'

Her face pale, she shook her head angrily. 'Don't be ridiculous! I'm paying the rent.'

'With the money from this job he invented for you, I suppose?' Oliver sneered.

'With the money I shall be earning, yes, and Matt didn't invent a job. He needs a secretary, you always said so.'

'Damn what I always said! If he wants a secretary, he can get someone else. He isn't getting my wife!' Oliver's voice thickened, his face becoming a sculptured mask: stone features hard and uncompromising, eyes so cold that they burned. 'How long has it been going on, that's all I want to know? How many years, behind my back?'

'For Pete's sake, Oliver,' Matt said unhappily, getting to his feet but staying well out of range of Oliver's fists. 'You can't really believe that I...that Fran...would do that to you?'

Oliver ran a hand through his black hair and Francesca suddenly realised it was wet; it was raining in the streets but she hadn't heard the sound of rain drumming on the windows until now, when she looked at Oliver's rain-wet hair and at that instant heard the sad, troubling sound of rain outside.

'Why not? It happens every day—some poor bastard finding out that his wife is sleeping with the swine he thought was his best friend!'

Francesca looked at Matt's agitated face and bit her lip. 'Matt, I'm sorry to have dragged you into this. I wasn't expecting anything like this, or I'd never have asked you for help. You'd better go. This isn't your problem, it's mine, and I think Oliver and I have to sort it out alone.'

Matt hesitated, eyes anxious. 'Are you sure? You may need me . . .'

He shouldn't have phrased it like that. Oliver swung round on him, teeth bared. 'You heard her! Get out of here—or do I have to throw you out?'

'Please go, Matt,' Francesca said hurriedly, afraid of more violence, but Matt was getting angry too, now. He had aggression in his eyes and was squaring up to Oliver, his hands curling into fists.

'I'm not leaving her alone with a violent bastard like you! When she told me she was leaving you I was taken aback and couldn't understand why . . . now I'm beginning to *see* why! I never had you down as the type to knock his wife about, but I can see I didn't know you at all. You're capable of anything in one of your vicious tempers.'

'What the hell are you talking about? Has she told you I beat her up? I've never laid a finger on her, but I'm damned well going to beat the daylights out of *you*, mister!' Oliver's broad shoulders were tense, his body stiffly poised to hit him again, and Francesca hurriedly moved between them, facing Matt, her dark blue eyes pleading with him.

'I don't want any more trouble, Matt. Please, I'm very grateful to you for sticking up for me, but I'd rather you left now and let me talk to him alone. Don't worry, he won't hit me; he never has. That isn't why I'm leaving him, but I can't be totally frank with him while you're here. I'm not discussing my marriage in front of someone else, so I must ask you to leave, and thank you for everything you've tried to do for me.'

Matt stared uncertainly at her, then nodded. 'OK, if you say so, Fran, but I'll sit outside in my car until he's left, and if you need me just give me a yell and I'll come running.'

Oliver's mouth went crooked with rage. 'You'll come running, will you? If you do, I'll be ready for you!'

Matt gave him an angry stare, but turned on his heel and left.

For a moment after the front door had slammed shut, Oliver and Francesca didn't move or speak. They stood there, staring at each other, and the way Oliver looked at her made her blood run cold. His narrowed, distasteful eyes moved over her slowly, from her flowing blonde hair to the casual intimacy of the caftan down to her stockinged feet. She had kicked off her shoes before lying down on the chaise-longue, and that perfectly innocent action now added to the evidence against her in Oliver's eyes.

'A pity I didn't arrive half an hour later,' he drawled coldly, his gaze lifting to her face again.

'I might have caught you in bed together, and you wouldn't have been able to lie your way out of that, would you? Although I can't see why you're bothering to lie, since you appear to have walked out on me anyway. Will I be hearing from your solicitor soon, or do you expect me to start divorce proceedings?'

'I have left you,' she admitted quietly. 'I suppose you got this address from your personnel department?'

'My secretary heard the gossip this afternoon when she got back from Wales.' He caught the lift of Francesca's head and his lip curled. 'Yes, the gossip has started, but then, that was what you wanted, wasn't it? To cause scandal, make me look ridiculous in my own firm? You walk in there with my partner and get taken on as his secretary while I'm away, and my employees all start whispering and wondering if I know what's going on! When Janice rang I was knocked sideways but, thank heavens, I had the self-control not to give away how surprised I was! I held my tongue while she was talking, and pretended to know all about it. As soon as she'd hung up I tried to ring you at home, but of course you weren't there, were you? The answering machine has been answering calls for days, and I should have realised something was wrong from that.' He frowned, his eyes lowered. 'Well, I did, of course, but I thought you were sulking because I hadn't been able to get home for our wedding anniversary. I suppose that was what pushed you into leaving?'

'It was the final straw.'

Oliver looked at her, his mouth impatient. 'I'm sorry, but I had no choice. I had to go to Wales!'

'I realised that. I'm not saying you were wrong to go, but I've had enough of the way I've had to live for the past few years. You're never home. Oh, yes, you always have excellent reasons for having to break dates, change arrangements, but what it comes down to is that I live in the country and you live in London, and we never see each other.'

His frown cut deep lines in his forehead, his grey eyes hard. 'So you turned to Matt for company, is that what you're saying?'

'I'm not having an affair with Matt! Will you leave him out of this?'

'How can I do that, for heaven's sake? I always knew he fancied you, right from the start, but it never occurred to me that I couldn't trust him with you. I'd have sworn Matt was too decent to make a play for you behind my back.'

'Matt hasn't done anything of the kind! When you didn't show up last weekend, I decided I had to get away. I came to London because I wanted to be somewhere lively. I was depressed and fed up. The more I thought about it, the more I realised that our marriage hadn't been a real one for years. I was just part of your window-dressing—like Lambourne. I was there to look pretty when you had important clients to impress, but you only came home when you brought guests with you. The rest of the time I was left down in Sussex alone, and now that Jon's away at boarding-school I'm completely alone, day after day. I arrange flowers and

sit on committees and help at charity func-
tions...but it's an empty life and I'm sick of it.'

His face had changed as she spoke, his eyes nar-
rowing. 'This has all happened since Jon went off
to boarding-school? I know you didn't want him
to go, and I can understand that you miss him. You
should have said something, not brooded over it
and cast me as the villain of the piece! I'll try to
get home more often in future, and there's no
reason why you shouldn't come up to London
whenever you like; do some shopping, go to the
theatre, or out to dinner. You're a free agent with
Jon away. I think that's an excellent idea,
and——'

'No,' she interrupted flatly. 'I don't want an occasional trip to London, and it's too late for you
to promise me that you'll try to get home more
often. You swore you'd be home for our tenth
wedding anniversary, but there was an explosion,
and you had to break your promise.'

'I thought you said you understood? I couldn't
help that!'

'I know, but it would happen again. Next time
it would be another crisis somewhere else, but
whatever the reason it would mean that I was alone
when you had promised to get home, and there
would be nothing for me to do but accept it. Well,
I've made up my mind. It isn't happening again. I
want a life of my own, I want to live it in London,
and I want a job as interesting and absorbing as
yours!'

Oliver's lips curled back, his grey eyes glittered furiously. 'Not in my firm! I won't have you working there!'

'Matt has given me a job with him, and I'm keeping it.'

'Matt had no right to give you a job.'

'He's your partner, he had every right.'

'I run the company, not Matt.'

'Do you?' she asked softly, arching her brows at him. 'Could you do it without Matt?'

'Of course,' Oliver said curtly, then his stare hardened. 'And what exactly do you mean by that?'

She smiled with mockery. 'If Matt left, the firm would be in trouble, and you know it.'

'Are you threatening to talk Matt into leaving?' Oliver asked incredulously.

'I was merely making a point. You and Matt are both essential to the company, and Matt has every right to appoint his own staff.'

'Not without consulting me!'

'Do you consult him before you make staff appointments?'

Oliver was getting very angry; his face was all bones, his skin dark red, his eyes points of steel. 'Are you trying to make me lose my temper? Because you're doing a fine job; just carry on like this and you'll be the one who's in trouble!'

'Don't threaten me, Oliver,' she said quietly, pleased with his reaction.

He took a step towards her, then turned and walked away, his hands clenched at his sides as if he wanted to hit her. She watched him prowl around, staring at nothing, until he came back to her, visibly controlling his temper.

'All right. What exactly do you want, Francesca? You seem to have made careful plans for your future—what plans have you made for mine? A divorce?'

'Not yet, no,' she said coolly, meeting his eyes without a flicker of expression in her face. 'I want a separation; we can make it legal, if you like, or wait and see how we both feel after a few months.'

His face smoothed out, his voice was level. 'And you're going to take this job with Matt.'

'Yes.' Well, he seemed to have accepted that now, anyway. So far, so good. Francesca didn't yet risk a sigh of relief; it would tell him too much about her secret uncertainty.

'And you plan to live here?' Oliver glanced around the room, his mouth twisting.

'Yes.'

'Alone?' he bit out.

'For the moment, yes,' she said with limpid frankness, meeting the dart of his stare. For a moment she thought he was going to turn violent again, then without another word he walked away and the front door slammed.

He had gone. She had won. Francesca sat down on the floor as if her legs had given way beneath her. She should have felt triumphant, but she didn't. She felt cold and frightened and very alone.

CHAPTER THREE

FRANCESCA wrote to Jon that night, telling him that she was going to be working in the company from now on and that she would mostly be living in London and had taken a flat. Her arrangement with Matt had been that she would take her time off whenever Jon was home from school, so she promised her son that she would still be able to spend lots of time with him when he was on holiday. She didn't mention that she had asked his father for a separation, nor did she breathe a word about divorce. Jon was too young to be burdened with such things. Her letter was carefully vague and she hoped it wouldn't worry Jon too much.

She rang his housemaster's wife next day and explained the change in the home situation, knowing that the school preferred to know at once about anything that might affect a boy's mental state.

'And what about the future?' the other woman asked, and Francesca sighed.

'I have no idea; I'm living day to day at the moment, but if Jon does seem upset over this give me a ring and I'll come at once, and bring his father with me. My husband doesn't want Jon unhappy any more than I do; we'll be able to put his mind at rest together.'

'Oh, so you and Mr Ransom are on good terms?' said the other woman in relief, and Francesca smoothly said,

'Oh, yes, of course!'

When she had rung off she made a face at her own thoughts—she and Oliver could paper over the cracks in their relationship for the benefit of their son, but it would be mere folly to try to deceive themselves that way. She curled up in bed in her hotel room, hoping desperately that she was doing the right thing, but plagued with doubts. It was a long time before she got to sleep.

Next day she was busy shopping for other furniture she would need: a bed, chest of drawers, a mirror for the little bedroom. In that room, too, she was only buying absolute essentials and spending as little money on them as possible. They were all delivered that afternoon, and by the evening she had moved into the flat. She wandered from one room to the other, faintly incredulous at being here, and yet satisfied with having achieved so much in such a short time.

She switched on the radio and began to get herself a light supper: a salad with cheese and some fresh fruit. She sat down at the little oak table, picked up her knife and fork, and jumped as someone banged in a peremptory way on her front door.

Oliver? she thought at once, flushing and dropping her knife and fork. She didn't know if she felt up to another argument with him tonight.

While she sat there, hesitating, there was another brisk tattoo on her door, so she got up and reluctantly went to answer it,

It wasn't Oliver at all; it was Matt, in a sweater and jeans. 'Oh, hello,' she said, and stepped back and waved him past her into the flat.

'Are you OK?' he asked, looking around the room as if checking that the place was safe.

'I'm fine, thanks,' she said blankly as he looked into the bedroom from the door. 'Matt, what on earth are you doing?'

'Making sure Oliver isn't here,' he admitted rue-fully, his shoulders relaxing as he grew certain they were alone. 'He put me through a meat grinder this morning. We've often argued in the past, but this wasn't an argument—it was full-scale war. I don't think I could face him again for a while.'

'I'm sorry, Matt, I didn't want to get you into a quarrel with Oliver!' Francesca looked unhappily at him and Matt smiled down into her dark blue eyes and hesitantly touched her cheek with one finger.

'Don't be daft!'

'No, I'm serious—it was selfish of me to ask you for help, knowing how Oliver was likely to react...'

'I'd have been offended if you'd asked anybody else! Don't worry, Oliver may make me nervous but I'm still glad you came to me, and I shall just tell him to go to hell if he tries to push me around again. Look, I won't stop long, Fran; I just came in to make sure you didn't need any more help here and to ask if you still felt you could start work on Monday.'

'No and yes,' she said grinning. 'No, I don't need any help, thanks, and yes, I shall be starting work on Monday.'

He smiled back and glanced at the table. 'Sorry, did I interrupt your supper?'

'I hadn't started it, I was just about to!' Francesca looked hard at him. 'Have you eaten? Join me, there's plenty of salad, bread and cheese—it isn't *cordon bleu* stuff, I'm afraid, but you're very welcome to share it with me.'

Matt looked at the food, looked at the door, looked at his watch. 'Thanks, Fran, it's a tempting thought...'

'But?' she asked with amusement as he looked at the door again. 'You have another date?'

'Good lord, no!' He laughed at that idea.

'Then why are you looking like a lemming wondering whether or not to jump off a cliff?'

He laughed again, looking startled. 'Is that how I look? Well, I don't know about the lemming bit, but jumping off a cliff would be a piece of cake compared to facing Oliver if he walked in and found me here again.'

Francesca wasn't surprised to find out what was making Matt so jumpy. She said coldly, 'I am not expecting Oliver.'

'Nobody ever expects Oliver, that's the secret of his success,' Matt drily said. 'He always takes people by surprise.' He turned to the door. 'I'm not a coward, but Oliver in a nasty mood can be very alarming, so I think I'd better go, Fran. I'm glad you're OK and everything is working out for you.'

She opened the front door for him, and on the landing a middle-aged man paused to smile at them both.

'Hello, are you my new neighbours? I'm from the floor above—Geoffrey Parker.'

'Hello.' Fran shook hands with him, murmuring her own name and adding, 'And this is a friend of mine who was helping me move in . . .'

'Oh, I see.' Mr Parker nodded to Matt. 'Well, I hope you'll be very happy here. It's a nice place to live, we're all friendly people . . .' His voice tailed off as there was a thud of hurried feet on the stairs, then Oliver shot into view and came to a standstill as he saw the little group outside Francesca's front door. Mr Parker gazed at him curiously. Matt stiffened as Oliver's narrowed gaze flicked over both of them before moving on to Francesca's face.

She lifted her chin in defiance, turned to Matt and said, 'Well, thanks for dropping by, Matt. See you.' He looked uncertainly from her to Oliver, but she didn't wait for him to work out what to do. She smiled politely at Mr Parker and said in a cheerful voice, 'Nice to have met you, Mr Parker. When I have a flat-warming party, I hope you'll come.'

'Love to,' he said, sounding fascinated by the changed atmosphere since Oliver arrived.

She smiled again, stepped back into her flat and firmly closed the front door. Safely inside, she stood there, listening, her heart crashing into her ribs, deafening her so much that at first she only very dimly heard what was happening on the landing outside the door.

'Well, must be off,' Mr Parker's voice murmured.

'Yes, so must I,' Matt said in relief.

She heard one of them going down the stairs, and knew it was Mr Parker as she picked up a low growl from Oliver.

'What are you doing here after what I said to you this morning?'

'I don't take orders from you,' Matt said, keeping his voice down so that she had to lean her ear against the door to hear.

'About my wife you damn well do!'

'If Fran needs my help, she'll get it, whatever you think.'

'If she needs help, she can ask me!'

'You're the last person she'd ask,' Matt said stupidly, and Francesca heard the rough intake of Oliver's breath. Even through a closed door she could pick up the waves of hostility between the men, and she couldn't let Matt get into a fight with Oliver over her, so she pulled the door open and both of them looked round at her, their faces dark red, their eyes belligerent.

'Matt, please go—I want to talk to Oliver,' she said, and Matt frowned at her, hesitating. 'Please, Matt,' she begged, and he shrugged and walked away down the stairs.

Oliver moved towards her but she barred the way, listening to the slam of the outer door as Matt left the building.

'I'm not inviting you into my home, Oliver,' she said coolly once she was sure Matt had gone, her blue eyes lifting to meet the grey stab of his.

'Your home?' The phrase seemed to infuriate him; his nostrils flared and his mouth hardened into a straight line as he stared at her.

'From now on, yes!' she said, staring back and refusing to be intimidated.

His lips unclamped enough for him to mutter icily, 'Well? You said you wanted to talk to me.'

'Yes, I do, about Matt . . .'

'I'm not discussing another man out here where anyone could overhear us!' he bit out, then took her arm in iron fingers, and before she could stop him, had thrust her backwards into the flat.

Francesca wrenched herself free with fury and saw the glint of satisfaction in his eyes. He was pleased with himself for having forced his will on her! That made her so angry, she turned on him, hoarsely shouting, 'Yes, you enjoy pushing people around, don't you? That's what you've been doing to Matt—threatening him with all sorts of reprisals for helping me!'

Oliver slammed the front door behind them. 'He has no business coming between me and my wife!'

'He's done nothing of the kind. I left you and came up to London without Matt knowing anything about it. Don't try to kid yourself that Matt has caused the break-up of our marriage, because it's not true. If Matt didn't exist, I would still have left you.'

A lightning flash of rage shot from his eyes and she backed into the sitting-room, her heart in her mouth. Oliver followed her in a tense prowl that held all the threat of a jungle animal tracking prey. Francesca felt her nerves crackling like a forest fire, but by the time she turned to face him again she had got herself under control once more, her dark blue eyes cool as they surveyed him.

She couldn't doubt his anger because she had left him, but how much wounded ego, hurt pride was involved? How much did he really care about her? Those were questions she did not intend to ask him, even if she ached to know the answers. She had meant to shock and startle him by her sudden decision to go; his reaction didn't surprise her, it was what she had been expecting, knowing Oliver.

What she didn't yet know was whether or not she had shaken him into looking at their marriage with new eyes. Time and habit had blurred their relationship; Oliver hadn't really seen her for years— was he 'seeing' her now? Did it matter to him that he was losing her, or was he in such a temper simply because one of his possessions was apparently walking out of the door?

Quietly, she said, 'Just stop picking rows with Matt, that's all. Oh, there's another thing... I've written to Jon...'

Another flash of rage, and her body tensed as he reached out to grab her.

'You've done what?' he snarled. 'I don't want Jon dragged into this squalid business.'

'Don't shout at me! And anyway, I was very careful what I said... just told him that I would be working in the company from now on, and that I was going to live in London during term-time. I'd already discussed holidays with Matt and arranged that whenever Jon was home I'd be free to look after him.'

'In this little box of a place?' sneered Oliver, his gaze shooting around the room in contempt.

'He might find it fun to sleep on the chaise-longue for a few nights,' she said, looking away.

'Lambourne is his home and that is where he'll spend his holidays!' Oliver insisted. 'If you want to see him, you'll have to do so at Lambourne.'

'You don't hold all the cards, Oliver, so don't imagine you do!' Francesca lifted her head to stare angrily at him. 'Don't force me to make this a legal fight for custody of Jon. He would be the one who suffered most from that.'

'Don't threaten me, Francesca!'

'You're the one who goes in for threats. I want a sensible compromise...'

'Compromise?' The word was spat at her; his hands tightened, biting into her flesh, and he shook her backwards and forwards so violently that her hair came tumbling down, the long blonde strands flying around her face and tangling in his fingers.

All the blood seemed to drain out of her face; she was icy cold and shaking one minute, and the next she had slumped in his grasp, her slender body swaying forward as her legs gave way beneath it. She didn't hear Oliver's startled gasp or feel his arms go round her, but as he lifted her off her feet to carry her over to the chaise-longue she began slowly to surface from that brief lapse into darkness and for a few seconds had forgotten where she was or what was happening. She lay there with closed eyes against Oliver's warm, breathing body, and a quiver of pleasure ran through her. She knew who was holding her, she breathed in the familiar masculine scent of his body, recognised the hand below her back and was aching with desire as he laid her down on the cushions and knelt beside her, pushing the ruffled hair back from her face, rubbing her hands, saying her name anxiously.

She kept her lids closed, afraid that if he looked into her eyes he would see the betraying passion in them. Oliver mustn't suspect that he could get to her that way. He was ruthless enough to use such knowledge.

'Fran,' he whispered, picking up one of her wrists, his fingers pressing into it. He was taking her pulse and she heard it then herself, thundering in her ears, racing around her veins. The rush of it seemed to double as Oliver put a hand on the side of her neck, feeling for the pulse there. The cool brush of his fingers on her skin was intensely pleasurable or she would have opened her eyes then, but how could she let him see what the caressing movement of his hand was doing to her?

There was a long silence and she felt him watching her; his eyes seemed to burn her skin, and she was having difficulty breathing. Oliver's fingers drifted down her throat and lay in the small, pale hollow just above the rise of her breasts; they slid downwards and with a shock she felt him undo the top button of her shirt.

She jack-knifed up to a sitting position, very flushed, her knees up to her chest, clasping them with her chin on top of them. She still couldn't meet Oliver's eyes, so she said huskily, 'I think you'd better go now.'

'You fainted,' Oliver said in a disturbingly silky voice. She could feel him watching her with bright, intent eyes.

'I'm fine. I'll be OK when I've eaten—it was just that I'd forgotten to eat all day and I suppose it caught up with me!' She wished he would move away so that she could get up, but he stayed where he was, much too close, and with that worrying look on his roughly chiselled face. She was afraid that Oliver had begun to pick up the sensual reaction inside her.

'You forgot to eat?' His voice rose angrily, and she felt his body tense again. Her body picked up every tiny signal from his; it was only his mind she couldn't fathom. 'How could you be so stupid? Even a child knows better than that. You've been running around London all day without any food inside you? And you want to come to live here, on you own? You aren't fit to do it.'

She bristled at that and was able at last to face him, her chin up, her dark blue eyes sharp. 'I'd have been fine if you hadn't forced your way in here and started bullying me!'

He had the grace to look confused. 'Bullying you? I did nothing of the kind!'

'You know you did. I fainted because you attacked me.'

'Attacked you?' His voice soared and his black brows met. 'Now you're being ridiculous. I gave you a little shake, like this...' He grabbed her shoulders and was about to shake her again when he met her eyes and froze, grimacing. 'OK, I'm sorry if I triggered your faint,' he muttered. 'Let me make amends. Have dinner with me.'

'I've got a perfectly good meal on the table waiting for me. If you'll kindly go, I can eat it.'

He glanced at the food and made a scornful face. 'That? Only fit for rabbits.'

'It suits me, so please go, Oliver.'

'You aren't being very consistent. You claim you left me because you saw nothing of me, but when I ask you out to dinner you turn me down!'

'Over the past three years the only times I've ever seen you was in public... at dinner parties, or receptions or balls, in London, and even in our own home only when you brought guests down to Lambourne with you. I don't want to see you in public any more, Oliver.'

He slowly ran a glance around the room. 'Is this private enough, then? Why don't I go and get some Chinese food and we'll share it here?'

She was tempted, but it was too soon. Every instinct warned her against agreeing. She shook her head. 'Not tonight. I'm tired. I want to have a light supper and go to bed early.'

'I like that idea very much,' he drawled, a glint in his grey eyes, and a fever ran through her veins, but she swallowed and forced a tight little smile.

'Goodnight, Oliver.' She was at the front door before he could catch her; she opened it and stood there, defying him, and after a pause he shrugged and walked over towards her, but then paused, looking down with tormenting amusement in his smile.

'I'm only going because you fainted earlier and I agree you need food and some sleep. Next time you won't escape this easily.'

'Goodnight, Oliver,' she merely repeated, and he laughed and went.

Francesca went to bed early, but she did not sleep well; she dreamt all night, erotic and sensuous dreams which she remembered with confusion in the morning. It must have been the cheese, she told herself. Cheese was notorious for disturbing sleep patterns.

She looked into her new mini-refrigerator and decided she had to buy some food that morning. All she had at the moment was the barest essentials, and if Oliver was going to drop in for supper unexpectedly over the weekend she wanted to have something special to offer him.

She would get some smoked salmon and fillet steak. It seemed an age since she'd cooked for him. When they were first married and living in their poky little flat she had loved cooking his meals, buying his food as thriftily as possible. She had been happy to walk a couple of miles to buy the cheapest cuts of meat which she would then spend hours tenderising and cooking slowly so that they tasted as good as the most expensive steak, and she haunted markets to buy the freshest vegetables at the lowest prices. She sighed with regret. Oliver had become accustomed to the best, in food as in everything else, and perhaps that applied to the women in his life, too? She had become too everyday and dull for him. It looked as if Oliver now preferred a woman as glitzy and spectacular as Janice Sylvester.

Pain made her close her eyes and bite down on her lip to stop the cry which tried to escape. Stop it! she ordered herself. She had already faced this possibility—why else was she here? But, so far, she couldn't be sure how Oliver really felt. He had been so angry when he'd found out that she proposed to leave him and live alone in London, work for the firm! Yet his rage did not mean he still loved her, nor did it prove that he was not having an affair with someone else. She had to be certain how Oliver really felt, what he really wanted, before she made up her mind what to do.

She wasn't about to make a fool of herself by asking Oliver outright. She was going to find out for herself. If Oliver was having an affair with that woman, she would soon know; once she saw the two of them together it would be blatantly obvious to her. After all, she had been married to Oliver for ten years and she knew so much about him, even if recently she had begun to think he had changed radically, was a different man from the one she had married. She might no longer be sure what he was thinking, but her body still vibrated to the music of his, and that was what would tell her if Oliver was making love to someone else.

Of course, she would pick up other evidence. There was bound to be gossip in the firm; she had seen from Matt's face that he suspected it, but he was far too loyal to tell her anything—not that she would ask him to betray Oliver. That wouldn't be fair. Men had these schoolboy codes; a wise woman understood and didn't upset their tribal attitudes. At times they seemed to her almost simple-minded, but nothing was ever that simple.

She wasn't simple, either, although Oliver had apparently begun to think she was. Both her actions and her motives at the moment were very

complex; she had decided to come to London partly
to find out the truth about Oliver and his secretary,
but partly for the reasons she had given both men.
Now that Jon wasn't at home most of the time,
there was nobody in the house all week. Nobody
needed her, and a woman had to feel needed.

Matt rang as she was about to go shopping. 'I
just thought you might like to know Oliver has had
to fly to Glasgow,' he said, obviously believing that
he was giving her very welcome news. It was as well
he couldn't see her face.

'Not another explosion?' she asked, her voice
slightly rough.

'Some union trouble on the building site of the
new Scottish factory. He may be away a few days.
What do you plan to do this weekend, Fran? I
thought I might drive through Windsor Safari Park,
have lunch somewhere around there, on the river.
Will you join me?'

'That's very kind, Matt, and some other time I'd
love to, but I have to go down to Lambourne to
sort various things out.' She had just made up her
mind to do that, in truth. She didn't want Matt to
get into the habit of asking her out, and this let
him down lightly for the moment, but in addition,
with Oliver hundreds of miles away it would be
quite safe for her to go back to their house for the
weekend without being afraid he would arrive there
too.

'Could I drive you?' suggested Matt at once, but
she gently said that she had her own car and,
anyway, she had too much to do down there to be
able to entertain guests. Matt reluctantly accepted

her decision and rang off, saying he would see her on Monday, then.

The roads leading to the Sussex coast were as crowded as ever, and it took Francesca several hours to reach her home. Lambourne looked so beautiful in the autumn sunlight that her spirits rose a little, but her disappointment because Oliver had flown off to Scotland lay on her chest like a stone as she went upstairs to her bedroom and sorted through her clothes to decide which she would take back to London with her.

She packed several cases and then had lunch in the kitchen, picking out a tin of vegetable soup which she ate with some crispbreads, followed by an apple she picked from one of their own trees in the little orchard at the bottom of the garden, and a small piece of Cheddar cheese from the refrigerator.

The house was immaculate; Mrs Hine had not skimped her work while her employer was away, and when Francesca had finished her meal she washed up and tidied the kitchen again. She didn't intend to leave any traces of her visit for Mrs Hine to clear away. She wandered around the house feeling lonely, and stood in her son's room, wishing Jon was there, touching his neat rows of books, his carefully arranged toys. Everything was outwardly so perfect; this was a glossy show-house—but it hadn't been a home for a long time and she wished she was back in London in her tiny flat.

She watched television that evening; it took her mind off other things, at least, and after a couple of hours of it she went to bed early, but couldn't get to sleep. She lay there listening to the familiar sounds of the Sussex countryside: the breathing of the wind in the trees, the distant cry of a fox, the haunting echo of a hunting owl somewhere nearby. She had adjusted to the sound of London traffic at night; coming back to country sounds was disturbing, and even more so was the darkness. In London there was always a golden glow, a sulphurous light in the sky from the miles and miles of street-lamps. Here there was only the light from the stars and a moon moving through cloud; the trees around the house made this a garden of shadows.

Tossing and turning, Francesca wished she had driven back to London. She hated going to bed in this great, empty house. She was afraid of the loneliness, the silences, the darkness.

Her body suddenly stiffened and turned icy cold as she heard a sound below; a creak, furtive, immediately stilled.

Was that someone downstairs, or had her own fear deceived her into hearing what wasn't really there?

She lay there, trying to listen yet deafened by the beating of her own heart, her eyes piercing the shadows in search of . . . what?

There it was again! Definite, this time. Someone was creeping about in the hall.

She swung out of bed and switched on her bedside lamp, her hand shaking as it groped for the old golf club she had kept there for several years, in case someone broke into the house. What if the intruder had a gun? She very carefully picked up

the phone from her bedside table and began to dial
the local police, then realised that she was getting
no dialling tone.

Oh, lord, he's cut the phone lines, she thought,
putting the phone down, then picking up and trying
again. Still no dialling tone. There was no doubt
about it. The line had been cut.

That was when she realised the creaking was
getting louder and coming closer. The intruder was
on the staircase. He was coming up here. She
grabbed for the stupid, lace-frilled négligé on the
end of her bed, and ran shakily to her bedroom
door, to push the bolt home before he got there.

As she reached the door, though, someone else
got to it, and it began to open.

Francesca threw herself forward, using her full
weight in a desperate struggle to shut the door and
bolt it. She was breathing rapidly, harshly, almost
deafening herself, except that she could hear other
breathing outside as the man opposing her used his
own body to push the door her way. He was the
stronger; she was no match for him. His superior
weight slowly began to tell. The door was gradually
thrust wider and wider until she couldn't hold it
any longer, and had to fall back, gripping her golf
club in one hand while with the other she uselessly
grasped the lacy edges of her delicate, more or less
transparent négligé as though to hide what lay beneath it.

'I've called the police!' she lied in a shaky voice,
her eyes huge, swimming with terror, the blue irises
very dark against her white skin, as her opponent
crashed through into the room.

CHAPTER FOUR

'IT'S only you!' the intruder said as he skidded to a stop and stared at her. 'I thought you were a burglar. You're lucky I didn't hit you first and take a good look at you second!'

The voice almost made her heart stop. She froze on the spot. 'You?' she got out. 'You?'

'Stop making owl noises and tell me what you're doing here,' Oliver drily said, sitting down on the end of her bed, his smooth black cashmere coat open over one of the Savile Row suits he liked to wear to impress new clients.

'Never mind what I'm doing here!' she bit back, incensed. 'The question is—what are you doing here?'

'This is my home,' Oliver murmured, the glint of sardonic amusement in his eyes. 'I never walked out of it. You were the one who did that, so you must forgive me if I'm slightly taken aback to find you back here so soon after telling me you had left for good.'

She flushed to her hair, her eyes hating him. 'I thought you were in Glasgow!'

'I was. I flew up there on the first shuttle this morning and flew back this evening. I meant to stay in London, but for some reason I decided to drive down here.' His eyes were wandering over her and she didn't like the way they were doing it. She clutched her négligé tighter, and Oliver observed the little movement, his mouth twisting.

'After ten years of marriage, isn't it a little late for such mock-modesty, Francesca? You're acting like a virgin schoolgirl.'

'Oh, shut up!' she snapped, glaring, and he laughed.

'What's the matter? Did I hit a nail on the head, darling? Do you feel like a virgin suddenly? I wonder why? Is it me or Matt who has made this miraculous difference to you?'

She felt like stamping her feet; rage was tearing through her and making her tremble. At least, she told herself it was rage. 'Get out of my bedroom!' she shouted at him, and Oliver eyed her through long, black, drooping lashes, mockery in every line of him.

'Your bedroom? Haven't you got your possessive pronouns muddled up, darling? This has always been our bedroom.' He stood up and shed his black cashmere overcoat, tossed it over a chair and began to take off his jacket.

'Well, it isn't now,' Francesca said, alarmed, but trying to hide it. 'Get out of this room at once, Oliver. I want to go back to bed.'

'Don't let me stop you,' he softly said, unbuttoning the sleekly fitting waistcoat and dropping that over the back of the chair.

'This joke has gone far enough!' she said huskily. 'I don't find it funny, anyway.'

'It isn't a joke.' He was undoing his shirt; she saw the gleam of tanned brown flesh, the wedge of black hair trailing from his chest downwards. She swallowed helplessly, a hot surge of sensual awareness hitting her.

'You are not sharing my room, Oliver!' She couldn't believe he meant this. Oliver might be a lot of things, but he had never been the type of man who would force himself on an unwilling woman, so this had to be an elaborate tease, but it was one which was scaring the hell out of her and she wished he would stop it.

'This is the room I meant to sleep in tonight,' he coolly said. 'This is the room I have always slept in. I see no reason for changing that just because you have unilaterally decided our marriage is over.' He had taken off his shirt now; he sat down on the bed again, ignoring her, and started to take off his immaculately gleaming black shoes.

'I'll make up a bed in another room,' she replied, moving to the door. Oliver didn't answer. He had dropped one shoe and was removing the other. Francesca looked back at him, biting her lip. 'Don't undress in here. Wait until I've made up the bed for you next door.'

'Not for me,' Oliver shrugged. 'I'm sleeping in here.'

'Oh, stop it!' seethed Francesca, marching back to him and grabbing up his neatly piled clothes. 'Come on, you are sleeping next door!'

'You can sleep where you like, but I am sleeping here.' He stood up and with a stab of alarm she saw him pull his trousers off.

That was when she gave up the struggle and fled, throwing his clothes on to the floor as she went.

Her mood was not improved by hearing Oliver laughing as she slammed the door shut.

Fuming, but helplessly unable to do anything about him, she made up the bed in the next room, hating him for the mockery in his eyes as he'd taken off his clothes. That had been a striptease with a difference. He had been tormenting her. Oliver might have been a remote husband for years now, but when they were first married they had been wildly passionate lovers, and he knew everything there was to know about her sensual reactions. He had known exactly what he was doing to her; he had timed it like someone throwing knives at a helpless victim.

She was so tired, too. She yawned angrily, smoothing down the duvet, and suddenly caught sight of Oliver reflected in the dressing-table mirror. He was leaning on the doorframe, his long, lean body now more or less covered up by black silk pyjamas, the loose Japanese-style jacket open to the waist, revealing the muscled power of his chest and shoulders. The very sight of him bothered Francesca, but what bothered her even more was the way he was watching her bend across the bed, her own body only too visible through the floating transparency of the négligé and nightdress.

Stiffening, she swung to confront him with enmity. 'Get out of here! Do I have to use violence to prove my point?'

He smiled crookedly. 'I brought you something you left behind in my room.' His hand came from behind his back; it held out the golf club to her. 'I thought you might feel safer with this next to your bed,' he mocked.

She wasn't going any closer to get it, so she just stared back.

He waited, still offering the club to her. 'What? Too scared even to come and get it?' he mocked, and at that she stamped over and snatched it. She wasn't letting him think she was that frightened of him.

'Very polite,' murmured Oliver.

Francesca said, 'I hope you noticed how heavy the iron is... any man who comes in here will get that over his head.'

'In that case, I'll have it for now,' said Oliver, snatching it back. He dropped it on a chair and grabbed Francesca's shoulders instead. 'You omitted to say thank you!'

Her pulses went crazy. 'Don't you dare...' she began in a helpless way, but his mouth closed over hers before she could finish the threat.

Her lips were parted as his kiss possessed them; she felt her treacherous eyes shut and the burning ache of desire begin deep down inside her body. Oliver's hands slid down her arms, yet at the same time jerked her closer so that their bodies touched, her skin beneath the fragile drifts of lacy silk becoming aware of the heat of his bare chest pressing against it. He was kissing her intimately, his tongue exploring her moist mouth. One of his hands closed on her back and forced her even closer; he slid a leg between her thighs and she couldn't stop the weak moan of excitement escaping from her throat.

Her head fell back, she felt his arm around her body, supporting her as he arched her over it. She was shivering, her mouth hotly kissing him back. She had one hand tangled in his hair, gripping it almost violently; her other hand was on his neck, caressing, fondling, moving down the smooth column of his throat to his bare shoulders, touching the ripple of muscles under that brown skin. As her palm pressed into his chest she felt the fast beating of his heart increasing, growing louder and louder. He slid the négligé off her shoulders and it floated to the floor. She felt the frail straps of her night-dress fall down over her arms. Oliver bent his head and his mouth touched her naked breast, his tongue hot and wet on her hard nipple. She stood, trembling, her eyes opening, dark as violets under her pale lids, her mouth swollen and rose-pink from the force of his kisses. He was softly sucking at her nipples and his hands were still busy; her night-dress was slipping down, down.

In the mirror she saw them both; her eyes, darkened with pleasure and hunger, saw the two bodies entangled, the female now naked, her skin glimmering and smooth, the male half clothed, his body hard with desire.

If he was having an affair with another woman, could he make love to her like this? Francesca thought on a wave of helplessness. He might have put his work first, been so busy that he forgot about her for days on end, but he must still love her, after all, and the shock of finding that she had left him had changed him, surely?

Oliver picked her up in his arms and swung towards the bed, and she let her arms go round his neck, yielding, her body warm and trembling against him.

As Oliver put her down on the bed a sudden noise made them both jump. Oliver straightened, his head lifting to listen, then he looked down at her, his eyes glittering, a black frown pulling his brows together.

'Who the hell is that?'

'It was the doorbell,' Francesca said blankly.

'I know that!' Oliver snapped as the bell rang again, louder and for longer this time. 'Who were you expecting?' he asked between his teeth, and she stared up at him without understanding what he meant at first.

'I wasn't expecting anyone!' Then she looked dazedly at the bedside clock. It was nearly two o'clock in the morning. She turned her blue eyes back to Oliver's scowling face and realised what he had been implying. She went red. 'What do you mean, who was I expecting?'

'You know who I meant!'

'No, I don't. I'm not in the habit of inviting anyone to call in the middle of the night.'

The bell rang again, even louder. Oliver glared at her, tying the wide sash of his Japanese pyjamas as he stood erect by the bed, pugnacity in the jut of his jaw.

'It won't be Matt, then?' The question had the sting of sarcasm.

'No, it won't!' Francesca had forgotten she was naked until that moment, as icy grey eyes raked contemptuously over her from head to foot. Having been reminded, though, she clutched at the duvet and wound herself into it with trembling hands while he watched her, his lip curling.

'Who else would come here at this hour?'

She looked at him with dislike. 'Why don't you answer it and find out? Whoever it is obviously has no intention of going away.' Far from it; the ringing was almost continuous now, and she could hear someone banging on the door panels too.

Oliver turned on his heel and went, and Francesca leapt off the bed and put on her nightdress and négligé, then tiptoed to the door to listen. Oliver was walking across the hall to the front door. She heard him open it, heard a man's voice speaking, but couldn't quite distinguish the actual words.

One thing she was certain about, it wasn't Matt. The voice was vaguely familiar, though. It had a local burr.

She crept to the banisters and leaned over to listen, and saw a dark blue uniform. She knew whose voice it was then, but why was the village policeman calling on them at that hour? His rumbling tones drifted up to her, slow and methodical, quietly soothing.

'Thought you were both away, sir, in London, not expected back for a while. I'd been keeping an eye on the place when I drove past on my nightly round, so when I saw lights I thought I'd better check. I had a look at the car outside, wasn't sure if it was yours, but as there were lights in various rooms I felt I should just make sure nothing was wrong. Sorry to have disturbed you.'

'Not at all, Officer,' Oliver said in a carefully polite voice. 'I'm grateful to you for taking so much trouble to protect my house.'

Francesca tiptoed away from the stairs, back to the bedroom. She closed the door softly, and then she bolted it. She got into bed and put out the light, then lay down, listening as the front door was shut again, noisily bolted. She heard Oliver's tread on the stairs, heard him halt outside her door, try to open it, fail, heard him breathing there and knew he was thinking, trying to work out how to get her to open it again.

He knocked quietly; she didn't answer.

'Fran, open up... don't you want to know who it was?' he asked, then waited for a reply. After a moment, he said wryly, 'It was the local bobby; he knew we were both away and the lights made him suspicious.'

Francesca closed her eyes and lay motionless.

'Fran, I'm sorry,' Oliver said huskily. 'I lost my temper, I didn't mean the crack about Matt.' He pushed at the door, knocked louder, raised his voice. He was getting angry now and she smiled in the darkness.

'Why don't you answer? Fran, are you in there? Are you OK? If you don't answer me, how do I know you haven't done something stupid? Open up, Fran, just let me see you're OK.' He paused and waited, but she made no sign of any kind, and when he spoke again his voice was louder and more furious.

'Do you want me to break this door down? If you refuse to answer, I'll have to.'

She refused to answer. If he wanted to do something stupid, let him.

He kicked the door, which shook. She heard Oliver swear in a muffled voice; he was barefoot and the door was mahogany. She hoped it had hurt. She laughed—and there was a silence outside the room.

'Damn you,' Oliver said, close to the door. He punched it and the panels shook, then she heard him walking away back to their bedroom. His door slammed; her door shook in sympathy. Francesca stopped smiling and lay for a long time staring into the darkness, her body churning with bitter frustration. Her only comfort was that Oliver must feel the same.

She finally fell asleep at around three, and woke to hear the birds singing in the autumn sunlight. The house was silent; Oliver must still be asleep. She frowned, biting her lip as she realised that her clothes were in the other bedroom. She wasn't going in there to get them! Then she remembered the cases she had packed and taken downstairs. She slid out of bed and put on her négligé, crept to the door and opened it. His door was firmly shut; she listened for a moment before softly making her way to the hall where the cases stood. She opened one and extracted some clothes, then made a dash to the bathroom on the ground floor and locked herself in there.

She showered and dressed quickly, then went into the kitchen to make some toast and coffee for herself. She was sitting at the kitchen table deep in thought ten minutes later when Oliver walked into the room. He was fully dressed, too; not as formally as he had been the night before, but casually, in an olive-green tracksuit. His grey eyes were needle-sharp as she looked coolly at him across the room.

'Going for a run?' she enquired, her coffee-cup clasped in both hands while she took another sip.

'Just had one!' he said curtly, and she should have realised he had been out. His black hair was windblown, all over the place; his skin had a fresh, high colour, and he was breathing roughly.

He walked over to touch the coffee-pot with one long index finger, testing its heat.

'It's ten minutes old, and not very hot any more,' she said, not moving or offering to make him a fresh pot, her blue eyes ironic as Oliver turned a threatening gaze on her.

'I want to talk to you,' he said through his teeth. 'I'm going up to have a shower, then I'll have my breakfast, and we'll talk this out. I'm not very hungry; just a boiled egg and toast, and coffee.'

Francesca didn't answer; she just took another sip from her cup and gazed at him over the rim of it, her eyes cerulean, innocent. He considered her for a second, then went out and upstairs.

As soon as she heard the bathroom door close, she got up and went out into the hall, collected the suitcases and took them out to her car. She loaded everything rapidly, went back into the house and up to the bedrooms to make sure she had everything she needed. She heard the shower stop, heard Oliver moving about in the bathroom, and fled, closing the front door almost silently.

As she drove out of the gates she glanced into he wing mirror and saw Oliver's face at the bedroom window. Even from that distance she could pick up waves of rage.

She was safely back in her new flat by mid-morning. All the traffic was going the other way this morning; out of London, down to the Sussex coast. The roads leading to London were half-empty and she made good time.

She rang Matt in case he took it into his head to drive down to Sussex.

'I'm back in London, and Oliver is at Lambourne,' she told him, and Matt made a whistling noise.

'When did he get there?'

'Last night, late. Apparently he solved whatever problem you'd been having in Scotland, so he flew back at once.'

'And found you there?' Matt sounded concerned; he was a very sweet man and she was grateful to him for caring. 'What happened?' Matt asked, and she lied.

'Nothing.' Well, as it happened, by sheer chance and good luck, nothing had happened, although if the village bobby hadn't been so conscientious it might have done. If he hadn't turned up at that precise moment she would have slept with Oliver last night, and her brief rebellion would have been over. She knew what that would have meant; she would be back in the same situation once more, and nothing would have been changed.

'I suppose Oliver was exhausted after a round trip like that,' Matt said. 'Flying to Glasgow and back, handling a strike, driving down to Sussex after landing back at Heathrow—and all in one day... I don't know where he finds the energy!'

'Neither do I,' she murmured, face startled, thinking of Oliver's intense lovemaking last night. After a day like that! It hadn't occurred to her before; she had always taken Oliver's ferocious energy for granted, but now she realised with shock just how extraordinary her husband must be. She had been so obsessed with her own erotic response to him that she hadn't thought about how he was feeling. Had he come back, highly charged, needing sexual release to bring him down after a day of tension and argument? Had it really been her he wanted? Or would any woman have seemed desirable to him?

'Have lunch,' invited Matt, as she might have expected, but she gently refused, saying she was tired after her trip.

'I'll see you tomorrow,' she said, ringing off, and sat for a long time staring at nothing, wishing she understood what made Oliver tick. When they were first married she had been too young to ask such questions; she had been crazy about him, had worshipped the ground he walked on, and whatever he wanted was what she wanted too. He was older, of course; she knew she hadn't been his first love, although he was hers. He hadn't gone into any detail, he hadn't mentioned names and she hadn't asked any questions at the time because she had been too much in love to want to hear about him with any other woman, but he had been frank about having had several love affairs before they met.

None of them had really mattered, he had said. She was the only one he had ever wanted to marry, and knowing that had made her so happy that she had brushed the past aside. Oliver was hers now, that was all that counted, she had thought blissfully, and set about making herself the sort of wife she saw Oliver wanted without once asking herself what sort of husband she wanted. Why should she, when she had the perfect husband already?

She had put Oliver on to a pedestal, she suddenly realised. She had accepted everything he said and did as perfect. She had never really seen him too clearly. How could you see someone who lived far above you on a pedestal?

It was time she did, though. If her marriage was to survive this crisis, both she and Oliver had to start seeing things in a very different way.

Next morning, she was naturally feeling very unsure of herself as she walked into the office building and presented the security man with her identity card, but on her way up in the lift she reminded herself that Matt would make her first few days easy to cope with; he wouldn't be a hard taskmaster. That was why she had gone to Matt for help. She knew she couldn't possibly deal with working in Oliver's part of the firm, among all those highly trained girls, most of them years younger than her, and all of them skilled and professional. She had had some secretarial training; she could type and do shorthand, she could file and do some bookkeeping and, thanks to her son and years of living with Oliver, she knew quite a bit about computers and would have no difficulty operating any of those made by the company.

All the same, she hadn't actually worked in an office for years. She had a lot to learn and would need patience from Matt. As she walked into the office she had a brave smile ready for him, but Matt was not in sight. Instead, she found Oliver's secretary sitting at a desk, rapidly sorting through a pile of mail.

Francesca halted, her backbone stiffening. Janice Sylvester glanced up, gave her a cool smile. 'Good morning,' she said, then pointedly looked at her watch. Francesca looked at her own. She wasn't late. It was just before nine, and Matt had told her to be there at nine o'clock.

'Secretarial staff are expected to be at their desks by nine o'clock,' Janice said in her honeyed voice, wearing that iceberg of a smile which always made Francesca feel like the *Titanic* trying to steer clear of disaster.

'It's just nine...' Francesca stared at her watch as the hands shifted '...now,' she finished as the hour registered. She looked up, offered Janice a smile a charming as her own. 'And I am here,' she said. 'But you are at my desk, which makes it difficult for me to be at it.'

'I have been sorting Matt's mail for ages,' Janice said, her voice implying that she meant to go on doing so, as well, in spite of Francesca's arrival.

'Well, now that I'm here that's one little chore off your list, anyway,' Francesca cooed. 'I know how busy you are. Don't let me keep you.'

Janice stayed in the chair, tapping her long, crimson fingernails on the desk. Her smile had frozen to her face. That made no difference to her beauty; she was too striking, with that luscious figure and flame of hair. Janice Sylvester was the type of woman who didn't like her own sex and was what was known as 'a man's woman'. She radiated sex appeal, but she had brains, too. Oliver had often said that Janice had a tough mind, and Francesca believed it. Those hostile eyes were clever and hard; diamond-sharp eyes with no softness anywhere in them. She used her sex like a weapon, Francesca thought.

'Before I go back to my own office, I'd better take you through the routine of the office. As I say, it's best to begin with the day's letters: skim through them and sort out any you feel Matt should see, ask if he wants to send an answer, take it down in shorthand or get him to record it on the dictaphone if he prefers to leave it until later. Type out any letter which must be sent at once.'

She took a breath and Francesca thought she was pausing, so she opened her own mouth to ask a question, but before she could get out a word Janice was talking again. 'Of course, you'll answer the phone and keep a permanent eye on the fax machine and on the various computers used for internal memos. If anything comes in on them, print out and file to show Matt as soon as possible; don't forget to make sure he sees any messages, naturally. You will also file anything Matt asks you to file, or leaves lying around, and he is given to doing that much too frequently. He has no security sense.

You must never leave this office empty unless every filing cabinet, every scrap of paper, is safely locked up. This is the nerve centre of the firm, as Oliver... Mr Ransom... always says.' As she said Oliver's name her eyelids flickered and she lowered them briefly, giving Francesca a quick glance through her lashes.

She did that deliberately, thought Francesca, her chest tight with jealousy and suspicion. She wanted me to know she calls him by his first name; that he isn't just her boss, that there's more to it than that.

Struggling to keep her feelings hidden from the other woman's watchful eyes. Francesca pretended not to have noticed the deliberate slip of the tongue, however.

'I'm sure I can manage,' she said, although she hoped she was going to be able to remember half of what Janice had told her. Janice had talked so fast, in such a brisk, clipped voice, without pausing to let her ask questions, but Francesca would have died rather than admit to this woman that she didn't understand every word she had said, couldn't remember all of it, or felt at all inadequate for the job.

Janice didn't want her here; that had been obvious from the moment Francesca walked in and found the redhead sitting at that desk. She wants me to fall flat on my face, Francesca thought. Well, I won't. I'm going to do this job, and do it well, if it kills me, and Janice Sylvester can take her long red talons out of my man, too. Oliver belongs to me, and it is time I reminded her of that fact.

She smiled charmingly at Janice. 'Thank you so much for all your help, I'll tell my husband how kind you've been, Miss Sylvester.' Looking at her watch she added, 'Good heavens, talking of my husband, it's nearly a quarter past nine, now, Miss Sylvester. He'll think you're late! You'd better hurry back to your own office.'

Janice Sylvester gave her a vicious look from slanting eyes, but she left, in something of a hurry, her curvaceous body swaying out of the door without another word from her. Francesca stared after her with dislike, grinding her teeth, then an idea hit her. She picked up the phone on the desk and dialled Oliver's internal number.

He answered on the first ring, his tone brusque. 'Yes?'

'Oliver?' She pretended not to be sure it was him, but of course she knew his voice at once, just as he knew hers.

'Francesca? Where are you?' He sounded surprised.

'In Matt's office,' she said, and quickly added, 'I just wanted to thank you for sending Miss Sylvester here to show me the ropes. It was very thoughtful of you.'

There was a silence, then he slowly said, 'That's OK. I hope she was a help.'

He hadn't known Janice Sylvester was coming here; he hadn't sent her, Francesca registered, although she had already guessed as much. He wasn't admitting it because she had rung to thank him, and like most men he was an opportunist, but Francesca suspected he would be curious about

Janice's motives, and that was just what she wanted him to be! Oliver might not realise exactly how ambitious his secretary was; he was clever enough where business was concerned, but he could be an awful fool about women.

'Have lunch with me,' Oliver said, and Francesca smiled to herself.

'I don't think I should go out to lunch today. I need time to get used to working here. I brought sandwiches and an apple.'

'Come up to my office and eat them with me,' he said at once.

'Sorry, Oliver, but I only have enough for one!'

'I'll send Janice out to buy some sandwiches.'

She laughed softly. 'Ask me another day.' She was automatically tidying a fine, stray strand of pale blonde hair back into her chignon, her eyes amused and tender. Men were so odd. Deny them something and they would move heaven and earth to get it, but the familiar and the habitual they forgot about for months on end. She was tempted to say yes; she wanted badly to see Oliver again. She couldn't stop thinking about what had happened on Saturday night. It had haunted her dreams for two nights, left her burning with frustration, but she knew she couldn't give in yet. Oliver still wasn't taking her seriously enough. She had to be firm.

The door clicked and with a start of surprise she looked up. Matt had come in and was staring at her as if totally amazed to see her there.

'Oh, I must go,' she told Oliver hurriedly. 'Matt wants me.'

'Damn Matt, he has no right to want you,' Oliver said in a harsh voice.

She laughed as if she thought he was being funny. 'Silly! You know what I meant! Bye.' She replaced the phone and smiled at Matt across the room. 'Good morning, boss.' Her smile was cheeky, her eyes dancing. 'You look as if you'd forgotten I started work today.'

'I had,' said Matt ruefully. 'It's so hard to believe it. When I walked in and saw you, I did a double-take.'

'I know. I saw your face.' Francesca had the giggles and Matt laughed, too, sitting down on the side of her desk and staring at her, shaking his head.

'This is so unbelievable—but I like it. Welcome aboard, Fran. I hope you're going to enjoy working here.'

'I'm sure I am.' She was determined to enjoy it; she was here to stay, and the sooner Oliver and Janice Sylvester realised that nothing was going to drive her away, the better.

CHAPTER FIVE

FRANCESCA rapidly discovered that, although Matt was under the impression that he did not have or need a secretary, one of the secretarial staff had always spent a few hours a day in his office; checking on the fax machine, the telex, the various computers around the walls of the long, silvery-grey-painted room. Even Oliver hadn't realised how much his own office staff had to do for Matt, they were far too discreet and efficient, but they welcomed Francesca with open arms.

Janice Sylvester might not want her around, but the other girls were delighted to have someone else doing all Matt's work, and they willingly helped Francesca to settle into the job. She became so efficient at the routine part of the work each day that soon she began to find herself with time on her hands. As she was not the type to enjoy being idle, if she had nothing left to do, she usually joined Matt in his workroom. He was always totally engrossed in whatever he was doing; and often seemed unaware that Francesca was in the room. His workroom had a long bench cluttered with keyboards, display units, a wide range of hard and software, and at one end a draughtsman's desk, at which he worked when he was getting his designs down in rough before transferring them to the screen where he could juggle endlessly with them with the magic of computer graphics.

Matt didn't sit on a chair so much as ride on one: a leather chair which swivelled in any direction and which had wheels on its legs. Matt straddled this chair like a horse and as he worked would slide from one end of his bench to the other and all around it. He looked to her like a little boy, whizzing happily around the bench, the tails of his white laboratory coat flapping.

If you spoke to him, he often didn't hear you. If you got through to him at last, he stared blankly as if you spoke a foreign language. When he was working, Matt was in another world. It could be infuriating, but it made him quite an easy boss to work for; he was no office tyrant.

Francesca was fascinated by computers, too, and soon got into the habit of spending most of the afternoon with Matt, at first as a silent observer and then gradually as an extra pair of hands. Once Matt got used to her presence, he started asking her for help in whatever he was doing, and very soon she was as involved in his latest project as he was.

Naturally, the rest of the staff were curious. She was their boss's wife and yet she was working for Matt, not him, added to which, Janice had made sure everyone knew that Mrs Ransom was not living with her husband any more. The reactions of the staff varied. Some women were sympathetic, others made it clear they thought she was a fool to give up such a luxurious life to work in an office. As for the men, they were either guarded and wary whenever they saw her, or they made a furtive pass.

She dealt with the flirts easily enough by mentioning Oliver in a pointed way. That got rid of them. Janice was not so easy to deal with.

She was becoming arrogant, openly hostile, because she was so sure Oliver's marriage was finished. She despised Francesca and made that obvious. For a clever woman, Janice was being rather stupid—it was always a mistake to underestimate an enemy. Francesca had no intention of making that mistake. That was one reason why she was here in London.

One lunchtime, Janice walked in and found several of the secretaries eating a sandwich lunch with Francesca while Matt was out on one of his jogging trips.

'What's going on?' Janice icily enquired. 'You girls shouldn't be in here.'

'This is our lunchtime!' Patti, one of the typists, said sulkily.

'And I invited them,' Francesca said, her chin up and her blue eyes dark with anger. She knew Janice was trying to humiliate her in front of the others. Damn her, who does she think she is? she thought.

'With Oliver...Mr Ransom's...permission?' purred Janice, and this time she was using Oliver's first name for the benefit of the other girls, rather than Francesca.

'I don't need to ask my husband's permission to invite someone into my office to share my lunch!' snapped Francesca.

There was a stifled giggle from Patti, and Janice's eyes looked daggers at her. She knew the other girls were smiling because Francesca had won that point, and she didn't like publicly losing a skirmish.

'They need to ask my permission, however, before they wander into a high security area! Mr Ransom is very insistent about security for the research department, especially when Mr Keilner isn't actually present. Other firms are more than capable of a little industrial spying.'

Francesca calmly said, 'Actually, it was my husband's idea that I should ask the other girls to show me the ropes at first!'

Janice stared at her, turning a strange shade of puce. 'Well, I suppose as you aren't really up to this job, even their help may be useful,' she muttered furiously. 'But I want them back at their desks on time, or there will be trouble.' Head high, she swept out, and Francesca laughed.

Patti looked worried. 'Fran, I know it's none of my business, but watch out for Janice. She's a nasty piece of work.'

Francesca shrugged. 'Never mind her! What were you saying about a flatwarming party, Heather?'

'Tonight, around seven,' Heather promptly said. 'Ted and I moved in at the weekend; this is our first real home. We've been renting a flat, but we're buying this place, and it's marvellous. Right by the river, on the Isle of Dogs; the builders only just finished it and we've got a terrific view.'

'Yuppie territory,' said Patti.

'Ted and me like it!' Heather informed her loftily.

'Ted's in the City,' Patti told Francesca, who smiled at Heather.

'That sounds like a good job.'

'Oh, it is. Ted earns very good money. Will you come? Bring a friend.'

'And she isn't inviting Janice!' said Patti when Francesca hesitated. 'So you needn't be afraid of meeting her there.'

'I'm not afraid of meeting her anywhere,' Francesca bristled, and saw the other two exchange looks.

'Well, you ought to be!' Patti said bluntly, and Heather said, 'Oh, sssh, Patti!'

'What do you mean?' Francesca asked Patti, who looked at Heather.

'If you don't like the way I tell her things, you tell her!' Patti said rather sulkily.

Heather flushed. She was a friendly girl with brown hair, light blue eyes and a very kind heart. She had been married a year, was in her early twenties, and reluctant to get involved in whatever was going on between Oliver Ransom and his wife.

Patti was eighteen and with no such inhibitions. When Heather couldn't bring herself to say anything, Patti blurted it out.

'Janice fancies Mr Ransom!'

Heather anxiously dived in, too. 'Nobody thinks he fancies her, though. Don't get the wrong idea.' She met Patti's round, childish, frank brown eyes. 'Well, they don't!' she argued.

'Men can never resist temptation,' Patti said darkly.

'Take no notice of her!' Heather said to Francesca. 'Mr Ransom wouldn't look twice at anyone else, I'm sure it's all just gossip.'

So there was gossip? thought Francesca, her heart sinking. She hadn't been imagining things; there was something going on between Oliver and Janice Sylvester. Humiliation stung in her throat. It was bad enough that he had cheated on her, but for everyone to know about it made it seem worse.

'Some people always want what belongs to someone else!' said Patti. 'Janice can make most men jump through hoops and she's bored with easy conquests. It gives her more of a kick to steal a man from his wife.'

'If she can!' Heather hurriedly said, an eye on Francesca's pale face. 'But she's too obvious about it, if you ask me! Mr Ransom's much too clever to be taken in by Janice.'

Both girls jumped as Matt loped back into the office, panting a little, his forehead dewed with sweat and his skin overheated. He threw himself down on a chair, groaning. 'I could kill for a cold drink.'

'I'll get you some water,' said Francesca, getting to her feet. She smiled at Heather and Patti as they edged towards the door. 'See you!'

'Don't forget tonight!' Heather reminded her, pushing a scrap of paper over the desk. 'That's our address. Seven o'clock. Please do come.'

'I'll try,' Francesca smiled back.

Matt glanced round as they closed the door behind them. 'Who were they?'

'Heather and Patti.' Francesca had got him a tall glass of ice-cold water from the fridge in his workroom. He took it and swallowed some, sighing with pleasure.

'Do I know them?'

'They work in Oliver's office and they've done lots of work for you, too. Sometimes I think you go around with your eyes shut.'

'Not in traffic,' he said, then roared with laughter at his own joke.

'You're just a schoolboy at heart!' teased Francesca, and he abruptly grabbed her by the waist, pulling her down on to his lap.

'Never say that again!' he grinned, his face just above hers.

She put a hand up to push him away; he caught it, stopped laughing, and suddenly kissed her palm. 'Fran...' he whispered, and she looked at him in shocked anxiety, realising that this was not a game any more. This was serious. She had never seen that look on Matt's face before.

Neither of them had heard the door open, but they both heard it slam. Matt's head lifted, he looked across the room and stiffened, letting go of Francesca, who could not stop herself rolling off his lap on to the floor. It was hard, and she gave an involuntary squawk as she hit it.

'I'm sorry, Fran,' Matt stammered. 'Are you hurt? Let me help...'

She scrambled to her feet before he got to her, staring past him at the harsh lines of Oliver's face. His grey eyes glittered in molten anger.

'Sorry to interrupt such a tender moment!' he snarled, and she felt like running away. Oliver's rage seemed to fill the whole room.

Matt swallowed, but didn't back off. 'I know what it may look like, Oliver, but don't jump to the wrong conclusion...'

'I'll tell you what it damned well looked like!' Oliver took a step towards him.

'We were only playing about,' Matt stupidly said, and Oliver breathed heavily, his hands clenching at his sides.

'Playing about? Is that what you call it?'

'Don't come in here throwing your weight around!' Francesca said fiercely, and he turned dangerous eyes on her. The back of her neck prickled with tension, but she defied him silently, her head thrown back.

'You seem to forget,' Oliver grated, 'you're still my wife! And this is my firm you work for! What if one of the staff had walked in here just now and caught you and Matt? There's enough gossip as it is, heaven knows! I don't want the whole firm to know that you're having an affair with Matt.'

'I'm not having an affair with Matt!' she threw back, enraged. 'Although if I wanted to have an affair with him it would be my business, not yours. You've been flying about all over the world with Janice Sylvester for years and getting away with it. You've no right to preach fidelity to me!'

Oliver stiffened, his eyes locked on to her and his body worryingly still. 'Janice?' he repeated slowly. Francesca stared into his eyes and saw an odd flicker in them. Oliver wasn't laughing off the tacit accusation; he was alert to what she was saying, waiting to hear more, to find out how much she knew or had guessed. That was why he was so good at business; he had a strong instinct for self-preservation, for picking up nuances, homing in on unspoken thoughts. He wasn't giving himself away or admitting anything yet. He was going to let her show him the inside of her head before he let her glimpse anything of what went on inside his!

'I'm not blind,' Francesca said hoarsely. 'I know what's been going on and I'm not accepting double standards. I'm not asking for any confessions, I don't want to hear about it, but just don't crash in here threatening me and Matt because you think we're doing what you've been doing for goodness knows how long!'

Oliver still didn't say anything, just stood there, eyes hard and brilliant, body tense, his face carved into an unreadable mask. She bitterly wondered if he was going to deny it; to lie. If he did, she would hate him even more.

Matt was looking uncomfortable, shifting from one foot to another. This conversation was getting far too personal for him. He began edging towards the door and Francesca quickly caught hold of his hand.

'Don't go, Matt. He's the one who's going.'

Matt threw Oliver a nervous look and Oliver gave him a chilly, menacing smile in return.

'I'm not going anywhere,' he denied. 'This conversation is just getting interesting. I suggest you go and change out of your track suit, take a shower, cool down. You look very hot and bothered, Matt.' Although he used Matt's name, it was in no friendly spirit; he said it softly, in threat, and Matt looked even more uneasy.

Francesca felt guilty; she was being selfish, asking Matt to support her against Oliver, knowing it would only cause trouble between the two men. They had, after all, been friends since they were children; she couldn't remember a real quarrel between them and she certainly did not want to be the cause of one now.

'Yes, you must need a shower, Matt, after that long run,' she said.

Matt still hesitated. 'Sure you'll be OK alone with him?'

'Do you want a punch on the nose?' Oliver enquired.

Matt ignored him. He said to Francesca, 'If you want me, I'll stay and make sure he doesn't bully you.'

'You seem to forget whose wife she is!' Oliver snapped.

Matt looked at him then. 'You're the one who keeps forgetting... that's why she left you!'

Oliver took a step towards him and Francesca hurriedly pushed Matt towards the door. 'Go and take that shower, and get changed, I'll be quite OK. I can handle him.'

Matt obediently left the room and Oliver stood there watching her with a crooked little smile curling his mouth.

'So... you can handle me, can you?'

'With one hand tied behind my back,' she said, chin lifted.

He laughed abruptly, looked surprised, then frowned. 'You've changed, you know. You almost seem like a different woman from the one I married.'

'After Jon was born you left me down in Sussex and forgot about me! I didn't stay the same all these years. People don't. I changed, but you were never there to notice.'

'That isn't true! Whenever I could get to Lambourne for a few days I did, but I was very busy. I was building the company, and I wasn't just doing it for myself, I was working for you and Jon, too. While I was slogging away in town, I liked to think of you and Jon at Lambourne, leading an idyllic life. Don't you think I often wished I was there, too?'

She laughed bitterly. 'No, I think you were having much too much fun up here in town!'

'Oh, for pity's sake, Fran,' he broke out, staring at her angrily, 'you don't think I was hitting the nightspots every night, do you? Or dating other women? Is that what this is really all about?'

'That isn't what I think, I never said it was! Don't twist my words, Oliver. I didn't leave you because I suspected you of living it up in town every night, and you know it.'

'Why did you leave me, then?'

'I've told you over and over again, but if you insist I'll say it once more. I left you because I rarely saw you, and when I did you always had a crowd of other people with you. I left you because our marriage hadn't been a real one for years, and I was bored and lonely and miserable.' She paused, her eyes angry. 'Come to think of it, I never really left you at all. You were the one who left me, years ago. You left me without saying you were going, you kept up a pretence that we were still married, but in fact we've almost become strangers. That's why I've changed without you noticing it. How could you notice anything about me when you were never around?'

'Give me a chance to notice you now,' he said softly, stroking her cheek.

'No, it's too late, Oliver!' She slapped his hand away, but he merely shifted it to her waist.

'You wouldn't have responded the way you did at Lambourne last weekend if you were indifferent to me,' he whispered, his lips brushing her throat, and Francesca shivered in involuntary response.

'I was half asleep, I didn't know what I was doing! Let go of me, Oliver! Someone might come in... Matt will be back any minute...' He was kissing her ear and the beat of her blood almost deafened her, but she fought against the way he was making her feel. It was not part of her plan for Oliver to make love to her every time they were alone. Somehow she had to keep him at a distance before things got out of hand.

'Ah, yes, Matt!' he said, his hands closing on her shoulders to hold her away so that he could stare accusingly down into her face. 'Matt...tell me the truth—what is going on between you two?'

'Nothing!' she protested automatically, but her dark blue eyes shifted away guiltily. Matt had startled her today. She had always thought of him as an old friend, someone she trusted like a brother. She'd never suspected that he might think of her in any other way, but when he'd kissed her hand after he'd pulled her down on to his lap he had looked at her differently, and Francesca was disturbed by it. This was something she hadn't bargained for!

'No?' Oliver's narrowed eyes probed her averted face. 'Then why were you sitting on his knee when I arrived, and why did you both look guilty?'

'We looked surprised, not guilty!' she protested, hoping she sounded convincing. She didn't yet know what was behind the way Matt had acted, whether he had just felt a passing impulse of attraction or whether something more lay behind that look, that kiss. One thing she was sure about—she wasn't telling Oliver anything!

'Hmm!' Oliver considered her, his face thoughtful. 'Another question intriguing me is why you chose to get a job in my firm. Why not work for someone else? There are plenty of jobs in London.'

'Not for someone who hasn't worked for years. My secretarial skills need brushing up; I need practice, and experience. I couldn't expect a strange firm to give me either. And anyway, why shouldn't I work for our firm?' Her eyes challenged him. 'You seem to forget how much I put into the firm for the first few years, both before Jon was born and afterwards, when I used to work while he slept in his pram in the office. I helped build this company. If we get a divorce, I'll be entitled to half your share in the firm, anyway, and I think the company owes me this job.'

Oliver's mouth twisted, he laughed tersely. 'Do you now?'

'Yes,' she said, head up and eyes direct.

He stared down into those deep blue eyes in silence, then slowly nodded. 'Maybe.' He smiled with sudden charm, the hard lines of his face relaxing. 'I have an important appointment in ten minutes, I'll have to go. Have dinner with me tonight.'

She felt her mouth go dry at the prospect. She was tempted to spend the evening with him, it was very hard to say no, but she said it, coolly. 'Sorry, I have another date.'

His face stopped smiling, became hard and dark and angry. 'With Matt?' he enquired, and there was cruelty in his voice, in the twist of his mouth, in his glittering eyes.

'With a friend,' she said, the hairs on the back of her neck rising at the barbaric look in his face.

Oliver was a hard man, a possessive man, a man of tenacious, acquisitive instincts which had driven him all his life. That was why he had done so much so quickly; why he had built this firm, put up new factories all over the place, acquired the firms of some of their smaller suppliers, bought and sold houses at bewildering rapidity until they ended up at Lambourne. He might not love her, but he felt he owned her; she was his property, and he would fight to keep her, as much to stop some other man getting her as because he really wanted her. The minute he'd thought he was losing her he had begun to fight to keep her. She wasn't deceived. That might be his idea of love. It wasn't hers. Oliver still had a lot to learn about love, and she was going to teach him.

'A friend? What friends do you have that I don't know?' he asked. 'Or is this someone you've picked up in London?'

'Yes,' she said coolly. 'Exactly. Someone I've met since I came here.'

'Who is he? Where did you meet him? What's his name?' Oliver fired the questions at her and she didn't answer, shaking her head at him.

'Stay out of my private life, Oliver. You've kept me out of yours for years; why should I let you into mine?'

'I haven't had any private life, damn it!'

She couldn't help a little spurt of laughter at his resentful expression. She almost believed him, but it wasn't relevant, anyway.

The door opened and Matt walked in, halting at the sight of Oliver still with her. 'Oh, hello...' he muttered.

'Get out!' Oliver ordered.

'Stay, Matt!' Francesca countered, and Oliver turned his grey eyes on her.

'Are you deliberately trying to make me really angry? You're going the right way about it, but you may be sorry when it's too late.' He turned and walked out, slamming the door behind him.

Matt stared after him, scowling. 'I've always thought a hell of a lot of Oliver, but he's pushing me too far! Who does he think he is, talking to me as I if were the office boy?'

'I'm sorry, Matt,' Francesca said gently, because she was very fond of Matt and it upset her to see him look so upset.

'It isn't your fault, Fran!' Matt said at once, smiling down at her. 'You aren't responsible for the way Oliver is made.'

'No, you are,' she said with rueful amusement, and saw Matt's face stiffen incredulously.

'Me? Fran, how can you say that? I . . .'

'Matt, Oliver's trouble is that he's made too much money, too fast. It's gone to his head. And he wouldn't have made all that money if it weren't for you. This whole firm runs on your brains, not Oliver's. Any competent manager or accountant could have marketed your products—only you could have invented them. Oliver has ceased to see that. He is so used to everyone he meets thinking that he's the linchpin of the organisation that he has forgotten how much you put into the firm.'

Matt stared at her, eyes thoughtful. She smiled at him affectionately.

'And if Oliver could hear me, he'd kill me,' she said, in wry appreciation of what she was doing.

'Yes, he probably would,' agreed Matt, rubbing a thumb along his chin as he grinned back at her. 'You're right, of course, and I may seem dumb to you, but I'm not that naïve. I know how much the company needs my ability to come up with new ideas all the time, but I also know that Oliver is a brilliant salesman and organiser. Fran, have you ever thought what would have happened if I hadn't set up in business with Oliver? I'd have worked for another company, who would have cheated me blind. All I've ever been interested in is my work. I'd probably have sold away my rights in everything for peanuts, without ever realising how much money was at stake.'

She nodded. He was right, he would have done, and there were plenty of people who would have taken him for every penny they could get out of him.

'Oliver has been fairness itself to me,' Matt said.

She met his eyes and flushed. 'I didn't suggest he had cheated you, Matt! That wasn't what I meant.'

'No, I know, I understand what you meant— Oliver has begun to think he's a damn sight more important than I am, just as he started to take you for granted, too. But it was Oliver who set up this company on borrowed capital which we repaid to the bank that lent it to us long ago, Fran. He has always treated me scrupulously, you have to give him that. It was Oliver who split the shares between the three of us, don't you remember?'

'The three of us!' Francesca's eyes widened and darkened, her lips parted on a gasp of shocked memory. She had forgotten that the share capital had been divided between all three of them right back in the first year of her marriage. Oliver had done that for excellent accounting reasons which had meant little to her then, since all they had been sharing was a large debt owed to the bank, and she had been so busy with having a baby later, and then with caring for Jon, that she had never thought of it again, apart from dutifully signing pieces of paper which Oliver put in front of her from time to time.

Matt was watching her, frowning. 'Yes, don't you remember? You own a third of the company.' He laughed. 'On paper, at least.'

'So I do,' Francesca said bitterly, realising at last why Oliver was so desperate not to let her go. She owned a third of the company; he could not afford to divorce her or he would risk losing financial control. She had begun to hope that Oliver still loved her even if he had been having some sort of secret relationship with Janice Sylvester. He had been so disturbed by talk of a divorce; what else was she to think?

'What's the matter?' asked Matt, puzzled by the wild misery in her blue eyes. 'Fran, what on earth is wrong?'

'I'm a fool, a blind, naïve fool,' she said, angry with herself, then she met Matt's bewildered stare and sighed. There was no point in explaining to Matt; he was as much one of Oliver's victims as she was!

'I wish I knew what you were talking about,' Matt said.

'Never mind.' Francesca grimaced. 'Matt, are you doing anything tonight? Feel like a party?'

His face brightened. 'With you? Any time.'

She laughed, then looked quickly at him, her eyes uncertain—he had been joking, hadn't he?

Half seriously, she said, 'I hope I'm not going to have trouble with you too!'

Matt laughed, then frowned as he thought over what she had said. 'What do you mean, me too? Who has been making a nuisance of himself?'

'I like the quick way you jump to conclusions!' She met his searching stare and smiled ruefully at him. 'Don't worry, I can cope with them all. It's all this gossip...some of the men seem to think I'm in desperate need of some male company now that I've split up with Oliver.'

'Damn cheek!' Matt exploded, bristling. 'Tell me who and I'll soon knock some sense into them.'

'You won't need to...I just gently dropped a hint that Oliver wouldn't like it, and they melted away into thin air.' She gave him a mischievous smile. 'You see, even Oliver has his uses!'

CHAPTER SIX

HEATHER'S new flat was ultra-modern and really far too small for the number of people who had crammed into it for the party. When Francesca and Matt arrived before the rest of the crowd, Heather proudly showed them round. It didn't take long—you could walk round the flat and see everything in two minutes—but Heather was thrilled to bits with everything in the place, and Francesca envied her that happy glow. She remembered how it had felt, ten years ago, when she and Oliver had moved into that poky little flat with a wonderful view of gasworks and endless roofs and chimneys.

'It's lovely,' she said to Heather, who beamed.

'Well, at least it's our own, and it's a start.'

'You'll be as happy as larks in it,' Francesca said, then the first wave of people arrived and she and Matt were soon boxed into a corner, a glass in one hand and something slightly odd on a cocktail stick in the other, talking to vaguely familiar people about the weather, the latest hit in the West End, a serial running on TV.

At one point she whispered to Matt, 'When we first arrived, I thought how tiny the flat was—have you counted heads lately? I'd swear there were fifty people in this room alone. Now I know how a sardine feels in a can.'

'Shall we go?' Matt asked, raising his voice above the thump and wail of the music Ted had just put on his music system.

'If we can fight our way to the door!' she shouted back, thinking that it was just as well that nobody else, as yet, had moved into the other flats in this newly erected block. Heather and Ted had no neighbours to complain, but the noise was deafening.

Matt pushed and shoved to clear a path for them, and they finally reached the front door again only to find themselves confronting Oliver and Janice Sylvester, who were just arriving. Oliver was removing Janice's short white mink jacket; she was glancing back at him over her shoulder, her red mouth curved in an alluring smile. Neither of them had noticed Francesca yet.

Matt gave her a concerned glance and she shrugged at him, grimacing. He was a very sensitive man, but she wished he wouldn't watch her all the time.

When she looked towards Oliver again, he had gone and Janice was alone. No doubt Oliver was taking her jacket into the tiny bedroom where all the coats had been laid. Francesca moved hurriedly towards the front door to escape before he came back.

Every man in sight was staring at the dress Janice was wearing; its stiffened black satin cups half covered her breasts, but her shoulders and arms were left bare. The rest of the dress was moulded to her like a sleek black skin, and above it her red hair burned against her very white skin. Francesca couldn't deny that Janice looked sexy and classy all in one; she wished she could, but she couldn't.

Janice saw her a second later, gave her a triumphant look and said softly, 'Hello, Matt,' kissing his cheek.

Matt looked taken aback, as if Janice had never kissed him before.

'Is it a fun party?' Janice asked the air between the two of them. She had not greeted Francesca, except to run a disparaging look over her. It was Matt who politely mumbled something about having a great time.

'We have to go, though,' he said. 'Can't find Ted or Heather! Will you say goodbye to them for us? We have to rush, we're...' His invention ran out and he looked blank. Janice's smile widened, her eyes cat-bright.

'Going out to supper together? How sweet. Of course I'll make sure Heather knows you've gone.'

'I bet she will,' Francesca said to Matt, as they escaped out into the crisp autumn night air. The block of flats lay at the end of a narrow street; just beyond it gleamed the river, black in shadow, or painted with reflected light from buildings and street-lamps.

Matt looked down at her, puzzled. 'What do you mean?'

'Janice will enjoy telling Heather we were so bored we walked out on her party. She likes puncturing other people's balloons.'

Matt was aghast. 'You don't really think she'd say something spiteful? Poor Heather... I'd hate her to think we left because we were bored... hang on a minute, Fran, I'll just run back and say goodbye to Heather before Janice can hurt her feelings.' He turned and raced back, while Francesca watched him ruefully. What a dear Matt was, and what a wonderful husband he would make some lucky girl, but the girl would have to do all the work. Matt was not the forceful type.

There were cars parked all along the road, most of the drivers probably here for the party. Francesca walked along to where Matt had parked and contemplated the way a red Ford had parked bumper to bumper behind him. There was another car right in front. How was Matt going to get out?

A footstep behind her made her stiffen. She swung and, with a leap of the heart, found herself facing Oliver, very tall and lean in a black evening suit and crisp white shirt. Only then did she glimpse the sleek outline of his Rolls parked in grand isolation right under a street-lamp for protection in this neighbourhood. He must have come out here to lock Janice's mink jacket safely in his car. With such a crowd at the party, it might not have been very sensible to leave it lying in a bedroom unattended.

He looked as surprised as she felt, then smiled. 'So this was the secret date you wouldn't tell me about? I'm glad I put in an appearance now. I was in two minds, but I gather it was expected of me, and I don't like to disappoint the staff on these occasions. Very exciting for Heather. Remember our first flat?'

She nodded, aware of the drift of his grey eyes over her, and wishing she had put on something more exciting than a rather simply cut blue silk dress. She hadn't wanted to outshine Heather. After all, this was Heather's big night, not hers. She still felt the same, but she knew she couldn't stand comparison with Janice in her figure-hugging black satin.

'I like you in blue,' Oliver said softly. 'I always did, remember?'

She flushed, her long, pale neck bent, the smooth, silvery chignon leaving most of it bare, and shivered at something in his voice.

'Cold? We'd better go in. It is rather chilly out here.' Oliver slid a hand under her arm, watching the vulnerable curve of her cheek with a smile in his eyes. 'The days are getting shorter. It will be Christmas soon and Jon will be home. Looking forward to it? I am. We may even have some snow; we did a couple of Christmases ago, remember? Jon does love snow at Christmas, and I thought I'd buy him a sledge in case it really freezes over and he gets some sledging on Hammer Hill. I wonder if he will have changed much. He'll have grown an inch or two, anyway.' He smiled down at her, urging her towards the block of flats.

'I'm not arriving, I'm leaving,' she said coldly, very glad she wasn't going to have to watch him with Janice at the party. Or, now that she had appeared, would he pretend to have come on his own? Would he give Janice some secret signal to stay away as long as his wife was around?

'So soon?' He raised his brows, eyes amused. 'Nobody there you wanted to talk to? Well, come back now, for a few minutes. We'll put in an appearance and then go to dinner somewhere special.'

She shook her head. 'No, thank you, I can't.' She found it hard to speak at all, she was so angry.

Oliver frowned, glanced over his shoulder at the lighted windows of the flat, from which a babble of voices and the crash of pop music came. 'No, I suppose you wouldn't want to go back after leaving. Look, wait here for me. I'll just dash in, say hello, and apologise for not being able to stay. It won't take two minutes, then we'll find somewhere nice to eat.'

She considered his face icily. When he said he was going to dash in to say hello and apologise for not being able to stay, what he really meant was that he was going to tell Janice that he was leaving her there and going off with his wife. Francesca would like to see Janice's face at that moment!

He hadn't mentioned Janice, to her, of course. No doubt he imagined she had no idea that he had actually brought the other girl here. Did he think she was blind, deaf, dumb, stupid? Or that other people were? How long did he think he could get away with an affair with Janice without anyone catching on? Most of the London office staff were in that flat. They knew he had arrived with Janice and they could put two and two together pretty accurately.

'I'm waiting for Matt, actually,' she told him in a flat voice. 'He went back inside for a moment, but he'll be out soon.'

Oliver's brows dragged together, she saw his mouth harden into a straight line. He shot another look at the flat's windows, then back at her remote face. 'You came with Matt?' he repeated, sounding incredulous. 'You actually arrived at an office party with my partner, not me?' He lowered his voice, but the note was just as harsh. 'What are you trying to do to me? Isn't there enough gossip already? What will people think when they see you going out with Matt, not me?'

'No doubt just what they think when they see you going to an office party with your secretary, not me,' said Francesca with bitter emphasis, and saw his face tighten, those grey eyes narrow on her face. 'Yes,' she said, 'I saw you and Janice arrive together, so you can stop pretending you came alone.'

'Don't be ridiculous!' he snapped, scowling. 'It isn't the same thing at all. I drove Janice here straight from the office. She would have had to get a taxi if I hadn't given her a lift.'

Francesca laughed sarcastically. 'Very plausible, except that some people might think it rather odd that you are both wearing evening dress. Is that what the best people are wearing for the office these days?'

'We both changed before we left, obviously!' said Oliver in biting irritation, his body tense.

'For a little office party? When you only meant to pop in for a few minutes and then make your excuses?'

A dark streak of red ran over his cheekbones and his eyes glittered. His voice had become even more incisive; he was barely parting his teeth to clip out his words now. 'As it happens, there's another party later tonight, a reception at the Savoy, given by one of our American contacts, a multinational combine who are interested in the new mini portable Matt has been perfecting. I meant to go on to that after calling in here.'

'Taking Janice with you, of course,' Francesca murmured, and got a furious glare from him.

'She is my secretary!'

'And rarely far from your side!'

Oliver's hands shot out and seized hold of her arms, his fingers digging into her and making her wince. 'I know what you're up to! Don't think I'm stupid. This is a cunning little plot, isn't it? You want a divorce, but you don't want your affair with Matt dragged into it, so you're trying to make it look as if you only started seeing Matt after you found out I was involved with Janice. If you can do that, it cancels out your infidelity, and the financial settlement will be all in your favour. If I'm not bloody careful, you'll end up owning more of my company than I do! Very clever, my love. Did you think that up, or did Matt?'

'Neither of us thought up anything! Only someone with a mind as devious as a snake's could accuse us of such a cheap plan.' His fingers tightened and she burst out, 'Let go of me, that hurts!' She tried to drag herself away, flushed and shaking with rage. 'If you think you can bully me into doing what you want, you don't know me!'

'You're right, I don't know you,' Oliver muttered, staring down into her face, then he bent his head rapidly and kissed her with bruising insistence, the power of the kiss forcing her head back until her stretched throat hurt. She tried to fight, struggling and hitting back at him, but that merely made him more determined; his powerful body overwhelmed her, and even as he hurt her she was shuddering with aroused pleasure in the contact, her breasts swollen and aching as he crushed her closer. The rage and hostility between them had turned into something else; more primitive, intensely erotic, a volcanic desire exploding through them both and making Francesca's head swim. Her hands attacked, and clutched, her nails dug into the nape of his neck, ran up into his black hair. Her body writhed as if in agony and she was groaning under the brutal demand of his mouth.

'I don't know you,' Oliver whispered again, hoarsely, without lifting his mouth from hers. 'But hell, I want you. I've got to have you tonight—come back with me now, let me make love to you, Fran...' His hands were sliding over her, caressing her back, her breasts, her waist, the soft curve of her hips, down over her thighs, and as he touched her his breathing thickened and grew louder; she felt him shaking, felt the red-hot brush of his skin on her own and triumph sang in her blood.

She closed her eyes to enjoy the moment, leaning on him. She wanted him just as badly as he wanted her, but she prolonged the ecstasy of frustration, the deep-seated ache of need. She would tell him in a moment, yield, go with him to relieve this terrible desire, but not yet. She shivered under his pleading caress, felt his lips trembling against her mouth, her throat, and thought how long it was since Oliver had touched her like this, wanted her with such hunger.

'I want you, darling,' Oliver muttered. 'Can't you see how much I want you?'

But another voice cut through that husky murmur; it was a cool voice, very self-confident, even arrogant, and the sound of it made the heated blood drain from Francesca's face, made Oliver stiffen and fall silent.

'We aren't staying long, either, we're going on to the Savoy,' the voice said from the steps of the block of flats.

'The Savoy? Sounds very glamorous. I've never been there,' Matt's voice answered.

Oliver let his arms drop, and he stood still, breathing as if he had been running, his grey eyes, darkened with desire, watching Francesca.

'Come home with me,' he repeated in an urgent whisper. 'Quickly, say yes quickly; we can get back into the car and go before they see us.'

She was as cold now as she had been hot a moment ago. She looked bitterly at him; he had made her forget for a while, she had so nearly given in to her own desire, but luckily she had been reminded in time and Oliver wasn't winning this round after all.

'Janice is looking for you,' she said, smiling coldly. 'And Matt's looking for me.' She didn't wait for him to answer; she walked away, skirts rustling, and the sound of her footsteps on the pavement made Matt turn, his face clearing.

'Oh, there you are! Sorry to take so long, I couldn't find Heather for ages. Stupid of me not

to unlock the car so that you could sit in it while
you waited—you must be frozen standing about in
the street all this time!'

'I'm OK,' she said huskily, aware of Janice
watching with eyes as hard as jade. 'I had
company,' she added deliberately as Oliver slowly
walked over to join them, then she slid a hand
through Matt's arm and smiled up at him. 'Shall
we go?'

'Sure,' he said, but gave Oliver a wary sideways
glance.

'Hello, Matt,' Oliver said curtly.

'Oh…hi!' said Matt, a nervous look on his face.

'Enjoy yourselves,' Francesca murmured to the
other two. 'Come on, Matt, I don't know about
you, but I'm ravenous.'

'Yes, OK,' he said, and they began to walk away,
only to find Oliver barring their path.

'I just had an idea. Why don't you two join us
at the Savoy? Francesca and I haven't celebrated
our tenth wedding anniversary yet, and it's about
time we did.'

Janice didn't stop smiling, but somehow
Francesca didn't think she was in a very good mood
any more. 'But what about poor Heather's party?
You have to put in an appearance or she'll be so
hurt.'

'I did put in an appearance,' said Oliver tersely.
'I said hello to Ted when he met us at the door, he
knows I came.' He hadn't taken his eyes off
Francesca; his stare was demanding, insistent, ordering her to agree to this dinner at the Savoy. She

looked down, watching him through half-lowered lashes, wishing she could read his mind.

Janice hadn't given up, she merely raised her voice an octave or so, trying to bring his attention back to herself. 'But we have to go to this reception in an hour or so, and it's vital that we show up for that, you said so yourself!'

'You can go and make excuses!' Oliver snapped.

'Oh, no, you mustn't do that,' said Francesca softly. 'It's very important that we sell the new Porta to the Americans, isn't it? Of course you must go to their reception and chat them up. If we make that sale it would bring in valuable dollars and open up an entirely new market for us.'

Matt nodded eagerly. 'That's absolutely true, Oliver. It would be terrific for us to make a big sale on the Porta. I've got high hopes for it. If I can get it right before Christmas, we can go into production with it early in the New Year, and it would help a lot to have a big order to fill right away, wouldn't it? That would keep risk costs down and mean we won't have any trouble with the bank with an overdraft to cover production. I've got a strong feeling about this one, Oliver. I'm ironing out the bugs without any problem, and——'

'OK, OK,' Oliver said irritably. 'This isn't the time and place for one of your rhapsodies about your latest baby. And anyway, you know nothing about marketing. Stick to what you do know, just do your own stuff and let me do mine.'

'Obviously you must go to the Savoy, Oliver, and we'd only be in the way!' Francesca said, her eyes limpid. 'Good luck with the Americans.'

This time he made no attempt to stop them, but he watched them walk over to Matt's car, his stare so angry that Francesca almost felt that it burned a hole in her back.

She settled down in the passenger seat with a sigh of relief, but the ordeal wasn't over yet. Matt still had to get out of a very tight parking spot. He gripped the wheel, grimacing. 'I'm as nervous as hell. I wish Oliver would stop watching me, he's making me jumpy.'

That was his intention, recognised Francesca, and he stood there, tall, dark and nasty, sardonically observing Matt's uneasy attempts to get away: backing and then edging forward, backing and edging forward, twisting his wheel with desperate heaves and groans. In the wing mirror Francesca could see Oliver, his black hair ruffled by the night wind, his eyes glinting. She could see Janice, too, frowning, impatient, trying to persuade Oliver back into the party. She wanted everyone to see her with him, of course; Oliver might not realise it, but by taking Janice instead of her to this party he was practically making a public announcement to the staff, and Janice feverishly wanted him to commit himself.

It wouldn't bother her that Francesca held a third of the company's shares, or that in the event of a divorce, especially if Francesca should marry Matt, Oliver stood to lose control of the company. Janice had nothing to lose and everything to gain if Oliver split up with his wife, and she was a very ambitious girl, that was all too obvious. She had been Oliver's secretary for several years now; she had worked her way into a position of trust at work, and Francesca was convinced there was a private relationship out of working hours.

No doubt she could find out for certain. She could engage a private detective who would dig out the proof for her, but she felt sick at the very idea of that. It would be too painful, too humiliating. She would rather not know for sure than pay someone to follow Oliver around and spy on him.

With a final gasp of relief, Matt at last managed to uncork his car and slowly drive away. She watched in the wing mirror as Janice slid a hand through Oliver's arm and leaned against him, her red hair a vivid splash of colour on the black of his evening suit.

Janice would lure him back into the party so that the staff could all see her with him, then she would talk him into taking her to the Savoy for this reception. And afterwards? What would they do after that?

'Well, where shall we eat?' asked Matt.

Francesca felt too sick to want to eat. 'I think I'll just go home, Matt,' she said, and he gave her a surprised glance.

'Oh, but I thought you were hungry?' He had taken her at her word when she'd talked about being ravenous. It wouldn't occur to Matt that she had only said that for Oliver's benefit. 'Why don't we go to the Savoy?' he cheerfully suggested. 'If Oliver and Janice can go there, why shouldn't we? As he said, you never did celebrate your wedding anniversary properly. Let's go and have caviare and champagne, Fran, live it up, enjoy ourselves!'

She was tempted for a second, then she thought twice and shook her head. 'We might run into Oliver when he goes along there later. No, I don't think that's a good idea, Matt.'

'Who cares if we do run into Oliver? We've as much right to be there as he has! Come to that, why shouldn't we go to this American reception? You and I are directors of the company; if Oliver is invited, so are we.'

'Directors?' repeated Francesca, at sea.

'Yes, you've been nominally on the board ever since we founded the firm. I know you don't come along to meetings, but you're still a director, as well as a major shareholder.'

They had left the East End of the old City of London now, and were entering brighter-lit areas further west. She saw St Paul's rising majestically between office blocks and stared with fixed eyes at it, thinking hard.

'That's something else I've forgotten all about, then. So I've been a sleeping board-member for years without doing a thing except sign papers? I ought to attend meetings, don't you think, Matt?'

Matt amiably nodded. 'If you want to, Fran, why not? I usually do, when Oliver reminds me, but it's only a matter of form. I leave all business decisions to him; he runs things like clockwork and there's no point in my interfering in what I don't understand. As he just said, each of us has his own territory and we don't overlap.'

She laughed. 'I bet he approves of that attitude.'

Matt grinned. 'Well, you know Oliver.'

'So I do,' she murmured, watching the street-lamps stretching ahead of them along the Embankment, on one side the black sheen of the Thames and on the other the towering façades of office blocks, the university buildings, the turn-of-the-century architecture of the Savoy, half hidden among trees.

'So, do we go to this reception?' asked Matt, slowing.

At that moment a sound reverberated on the autumn air; the deep tones of Big Ben chiming the hour. Automatically, Francesca glanced at her watch. 'It's nine o'clock, rather late for dinner,' she thought aloud, but Matt shook his head.

'I'm sure they'll still be serving dinner in the River Room. It isn't late by London standards. Oh, come on, Fran. I'm really looking forward to it now. It isn't often I have an adventure! It does you good to be impulsive once in a while.'

'That's true,' she agreed slowly. 'OK, let's do it!' She had acted on impulse when she'd driven away from Lambourne and come up to London. She had been taking a calculated risk, and with any luck it might still pay off. Why not take another?

'And after dinner, shall we go to the reception?' asked Matt.

'Why not?' She was curious about the American multinational which could be so important to them. She hadn't met one of their really big customers before, and if she was a director it was time she did. She must have been going around with her eyes shut for years not to have realised just how deeply she was enmeshed in the running of the company.

Oliver had been using her to rubber-stamp his decisions. How often had she dutifully signed whatever he told her to sign? She had never thought of reading the papers before she signed them, either. She trusted him so completely, and he had used her utter trust for his own ends. Her name was part of his machinery, just as the third of the shares she owned was part of his defence against a takeover by someone else. While she was his wife and stayed obediently down in Sussex, the arrangement suited Oliver very well, but now that she had left him she had upset everything. No wonder Oliver was desperate to get her back. She could ruin him, if she chose.

They dined at a quiet table in a corner of the famous River Room, looking down over the Embankment gardens to the Thames. Francesca was too tense to enjoy herself; she kept expecting Oliver and Janice to arrive, but they didn't, and when she and Matt left the dining-room she was half inclined to go home instead of going to the reception given by the American-headed multinational company. She even began to apologise to Matt, yawning slightly.

'I'm so tired, Matt, I think I'll go home.'

'Not yet,' he pleaded. 'Just another half an hour at the reception! I haven't had this much fun for years.'

She laughed at his boyish eagerness and couldn't refuse, so they asked at the reception desk and were directed to a large hospitality suite on the floor below. Matt surprised her by pulling out an engraved invitation card. He grinned at her expression.

'Well, it isn't often that I get invited to free booze at the Savoy! I put it in my pocket in case I felt brave enough to come.'

'Lucky I said yes, then,' she teased as he handed the card to the liveried flunkey on the door. The man gravely asked for their names, then as they walked past him into the half-full room, announced them in stentorian tones that made her jump.

Heads turned, people stared, and a man standing near by came forward with a warm smile, his hand outstretched.

'Mr Keilner? Matthew Keilner? Well, this is a great pleasure to me. I have been one of your admirers for a good many years, and I've often hoped to meet you when I was on a buying trip in the United Kingdom, but you were always tied up and I've only met your partner, Mr Ransom.'

'Thank you, Mr...?' Matt said, blushing endearingly at this frank praise.

'Garth,' the other man said, shaking his hand firmly.

'Mr Garth? I'm sure I've heard the name before, but I'm afraid I can't quite place it...' Matt gave him an uncertain smile.

'No, Garth is my first name. My surname is Abbey.'

'Good heavens, yes! Mr Abbey! Of course, I've heard Oliver...Ransom, that is...my partner... talking of you many times.'

Garth Abbey was a man of nearly sixty, faintly bald, with sharp brown eyes and the look of a portly cherub. He smiled at Matt with indulgence, as though men of such an original turn of mind could be forgiven for anything they said or did, then turned his gaze on Francesca.

'The master of ceremonies announced you as Mrs Ransom? Would that be Oliver's wife?'

She nodded, giving him her hand, which he took between both of his. 'This is a double pleasure, then,' he murmured, assessing her face and figure with a courteous display of appreciation. 'And very unexpected, which all the best pleasures always are. Does this mean that Oliver, after all, cannot make it? I spoke to his secretary this afternoon and she seemed sure he would be coming.'

'Oh, Oliver and Janice may get here later,' Francesca said, reassured by these remarks, but her dark blue eyes darting around hastily to make sure she wasn't going to look a fool. Yet if Oliver had arrived, Mr Abbey would not, surely, have asked her if he was coming? 'They were detained.'

'Oh, I see. Well, you are very welcome.' Mr Abbey clicked a finger and a waiter arrived with a tray of fluted glasses in which sparkled pale golden champagne. Mr Abbey lifted a glass, handed it to Francesca.

'A toast,' he said, giving Matt a glass. He himself lifted a glass ceremoniously. 'To your latest project, Mr Keilner. To Porta, a miracle breakthrough in miniaturised computerisation.' His sharp little eyes surveyed Matt's face. 'It is, isn't it?'

Matt's eyes glowed, but it was Francesca who answered, smiling softly. 'Oh, it is a miracle, Mr Abbey. This is Matt's masterpiece and it will be in production very shortly. It is going to sweep the board, revolutionise the computer world.'

Matt looked almost shocked; his modesty would not have allowed him to claim that much for his latest baby, much as he loved it. Garth Abbey studied his face, probing behind it for what was in Matt's mind.

'So? Is she right, Mr Keilner, or was that just the usual jazz—a big build-up for something not so very original?'

'Come and see the prototype in operation next week,' said Francesca, and Matt gave her a horrified look.

'Fran! Hey, now, we can't hand out invitations without consulting Oliver——'

'I'll settle with Oliver,' Mr Abbey said quickly. 'Next week? Which day, Mrs Ransom?'

'Friday?' she said coolly. 'That will give Matt a week to iron out any teething problems.'

'What will?' asked a curt voice behind them, and Francesca stiffened, turning slowly to look at Oliver. She was surprised to find that Janice was not with him. Had she gone home? Or was she here, but with some other group of people at the reception?

'What will give Matt a week to iron out teething problems?' repeated Oliver with clipped impatience when she didn't answer.

Matt began mumbling an explanation. Mr Abbey said something, too. Oliver listened to them, his face hardening, then focused his angry stare on Francesca again, his grey eyes icy.

She had made her first move in his private world; she had made a business appointment with a client without first consulting him, and, although he had been hoping to interest this multinational into giving them a huge order for Porta, Oliver was furious because she had acted independently.

His hard face and cold stare told her that she had trespassed on his territory, and warned her that punishment would follow, but Francesca lifted her chin and stared him out, her blue eyes defiant. Without a word, she tried to make it crystal-clear that she was not afraid of him, and he need not think she was! Of course, that wasn't true. She was afraid. She was absolutely terrified, but she wouldn't give Oliver the satisfaction of knowing that he scared the living hell out of her.

It was time she came out of his shadow and started making a place for herself in his world, whether Oliver approved or not.

CHAPTER SEVEN

Mr Abbey was a shrewd man and, like most men who ran big companies, he was an experienced tactician, not to say politician. He looked from one to the other of them, then smiled smoothly and took Oliver off to meet other people, giving him no chance to cancel the appointment to view the Porta prototype, or, indeed, to confront Francesca.

As Oliver walked off, Francesca couldn't suppress a sigh of relief, which he heard. He threw a narrow-eyed glare back over his shoulder as he went, so that she knew that the repercussions were merely postponed, they couldn't be avoided.

Oliver was furious! She had no illusions about what was going to happen when he got her alone. In fact, she was very lucky they hadn't been alone when he found out. Not that she regretted what she had done. After all, it wasn't as if Oliver didn't want a deal with this company. He didn't object to them seeing the prototype. He would undoubtedly have shown it to them if they had asked him. No, he was merely furious because she had had the nerve to make a move without first consulting him.

'Phew...' groaned Matt, fanning himself with one hand. 'That was a tricky moment! Did you see Oliver's face?'

'I saw,' she said, her gaze on the exit. 'Matt, I'm going, while Oliver's otherwise occupied.'

'So soon? Well, I'll drive you home,' he said at once, not sorry to be leaving, either.

'No,' she said hurriedly. 'Cover my retreat, will you, there's a darling? If Oliver looks round and sees we've both gone he'll be after us faster than you can blink, but if he sees you still here he'll suppose I'm around, too, maybe in the powder-room.'

Matt took on the look of a hunted rabbit, his nose twitching nervously. 'Do I have to?'

'Please, Matt!' she coaxed, although it was unkind to abandon him to Oliver's tender mercies.

'But how will you get home?'

'Take a taxi, of course.' She gazed at him pleadingly. 'OK, Matt? Will you stay and cover for me, make sure Oliver doesn't follow?'

Matt sighed in resignation, and she blew him a kiss.

'Thanks, I'll owe you one.' She carefully looked across the large, opulently furnished room to where Oliver stood in a circle of well-groomed well-dressed business men. He was watching her out of the corner of his eye. Francesca wandered idly towards the powder-room door, pretending not to have a care in the world, and vanished inside. As she had hoped, there was another exit, not into the hospitality suite but out into the hotel corridor. She raced through and was in a lift going back up to the ground floor within a few seconds.

There was always a queue of taxis waiting outside the Savoy. She jumped into one and was soon heading along the Strand, through Trafalgar Square, and then northwards to the suburb of

Finchley. It was late now; traffic was no longer so heavy, and although it was quite a distance from the hotel to the street where she lived it did not take as long as it normally would. Just over half an hour after leaving the hotel she was safely in her flat and in bed.

She didn't get to sleep for ages, however, because she kept expecting Oliver to arrive. By the time she did drift off, it was almost two in the morning, and when her alarm went she staggered out of bed feeling giddy and disorientated.

She rushed around, showering, getting dressed, drinking coffee, eating an apple and some yoghurt, but all the time she felt like an automaton. She had only had five and a half hours' sleep where she usually had eight.

When she reached her office she found that Matt hadn't put in an appearance yet, either. What time had he managed to get home last night? she wondered, going slowly through her usual routine with stifled yawns and a hammering head.

When the office door opened she looked up, expecting Matt, and went pale as she found herself facing Oliver, grim-faced, frowning, his eyes hostile.

'I want a word with you,' he bit out, slamming the door behind him, and she winced, her hand going up to her forehead.

'Oh, please! Don't make so much noise!' she moaned. 'I've got a headache.'

'Which you richly deserve,' Oliver told her, crossing the room to lean over her desk.

'Don't loom!' she muttered, finding his proximity unbearable.

He ignored that, his face inches from hers. 'How dare you muscle in on that operation last night? You could have wrecked the whole deal!' he grated.

'I didn't, though,' she said defiantly.

'Luckily for you.'

'There was nothing lucky about it. I knew what I was doing.'

'You've worked here five minutes, but you knew all about something we've been keeping under wraps for months?' snarled Oliver.

'Yes, that's right! Matt explained it to me on my first day here.'

'And of course you understood every word,' he said with icy sarcasm, and she glared back at him.

'Why shouldn't I? I was in on this business from the ground floor, remember, and I've kept up with what Matt has been producing all along. I do understand computers, Oliver; you can't say I don't. I knew how important it was for us all to sell Porta to those Americans, that's why I invited Garth along to see the prototype!'

'Garth?' asked Oliver blankly.

'Mr Abbey,' she explained. 'He asked us to call him by his first name.'

'Oh, did he?' Oliver looked disgusted. 'What else did he do? Ask you to have a little supper for two with him up in his private suite at the hotel?'

'Certainly not,' she said coldly. 'We talked business, nothing else.'

'That would probably have come later, if you'd stayed around, instead of dashing off with Matt.'

He glanced at the door into the workroom. 'I'll be speaking to him later, when I've dealt with you.'

'He isn't here yet.'

'Leave him in bed, did you?' Oliver asked viciously, and she threw him a furious look.

'I haven't seen Matt since last night. When I left the reception he stayed on. And I am not having an affair with Matt!'

'Then why are the two of you as thick as thieves?' Oliver demanded, and resentment welled up inside her.

'Why do you always have Janice Sylvester with you everywhere you go?'

'You know perfectly well that she is my secretary.'

'Well, snap! I work for Matt, that's why you keep seeing me with him!'

Oliver's teeth met; she watched him rage silently, staring at her, then he burst out, 'Well, don't you ever again take it upon yourself to interfere in a sales operation! Sales is my department. Matt is in charge of research and development. I don't interfere with his work; I don't want him, or you, interfering with mine.'

'And what's my particular department?' Francesca asked, opening her dark blue eyes at him, her long lashes curling back.

He looked incredulously at her. 'Your department?'

'I do own a third of the shares,' she reminded him, and he stiffened. She gave him a triumphant little smile. 'And I am a director, although it seems an awfully long time since I attended a board meeting. I must make sure I attend them all now I'm in London.'

Oliver had the look of a man caught helplessly in a net, raging and frustrated. 'What the hell has got into you? You're my wife! That used to be enough for you. Why did you suddenly get restless and want more than that? What's happened to you, Francesca? You're not the woman I married.'

'I want to share the running of our company with you and Matt,' she said coolly, and watched his jaw drop. 'The three of us started it in the beginning. I've been stuck down in the country long enough. From now on, I'm going to work with you and Matt up here.'

He was staring at her, his face all angles, tight with shock and anger. She heard him take a long, deep breath, then he asked sarcastically, 'That all? Surely you have a few more unreasonable demands?'

'Just one,' she said, smiling suddenly. 'Fire Janice.'

His face changed, his grey eyes glittering, wicked with amusement. 'Ah,' he said softly, and she eyed him suspiciously. 'You are jealous of Janice,' he taunted, and hot colour mounted to her hairline.

'Jealous of her? You must be kidding. If you want her, have her, see if I care.' She felt a pain burning in her throat like acid and her hands curled into claws, her nails digging into her palms, but she held her head high. She would not let him see just how jealous she was; he wasn't crowing over her. She hated the smile in his eyes. 'Just remember in future, though,' she grated. 'Anything you can do,

I can do better! If you want to be free to have affairs, that means I'm free too. You aren't leaving me behind again, either in business or any other way. I'm in London and in this company to stay! On equal terms with you!'

'Come back to me, Fran,' he said huskily, and her heart almost seemed to stop. He had stopped bullying, threatening, ordering. He was begging, and he meant it, but did he still love her, though? Or was it just the company he loved and was trying to defend by keeping her, even if he had to go on his knees to do it?

'It isn't as simple as that, though, is it?' she said, refusing to be hoodwinked. 'If we're to start again, you have got to re-think your attitude to our marriage...'

'I'm doing that now,' he said, sitting on the edge of her desk, leaning forward, a hand planted on each side of her head, trapping her in her chair. Confused, she looked up into those mocking grey eyes, and Oliver smiled slowly at her as he began to take the pins out of her chignon.

'You look much sexier with your hair down, you know...'

'Oliver! Anyone might walk in...' she protested, her face hot as she felt her long blonde hair tumble down her back.

He grabbed a handful of her hair and tugged to make her tilt her face up to him, leaning over her mere inches away.

'That hurts!' she said, but the words were stifled in her mouth by the hungry compulsion of his lips, the demanding sweetness which turned her bones to water and made her head spin. Her eyes shut, she lay back weakly and kissed him back, her hands clasping his face, the heat of his skin burning her palms.

He lifted his mouth and she opened her eyes to look drowsily at him. 'Move into my flat tonight,' Oliver whispered, a faint tremor in his voice.

She quivered, her mouth going dry. It seemed a lifetime since they had made love. She wanted him with an urgency that hurt, but she needed time to think. They still hadn't resolved the problem of his relationship with Janice, and until they had she couldn't trust him with her happiness again.

'What about Janice?' she asked. 'Tell me the truth, Oliver...have you been having an affair with her?'

'No, darling,' he said, kissing her throat with hot, pleading lips. 'No.'

She couldn't see his eyes to be certain that was the truth, but she wanted so much to believe him. 'She fancies you,' she said. 'Don't tell me you don't know that, Oliver.'

He shrugged. 'She's a damned good secretary, that's all I know, and I haven't had an affair with her, Franccsca! Are you going to believe me or not?' His voice had an edge to it now.

Sighing, she said, 'Give me more time. I need to think.'

'Think about what, for heaven's sake?' The edge had become an audible impatience; he was getting angry because she wasn't giving in at once.

'Us, Oliver,' she said, 'I need time to think about us and whether or not our marriage can work if we make a new start—and shouting at me or insisting on your own way is not going to make me feel too optimistic about our future together! I left you in the first place because you treated me like a doll in a doll's house. You put me into Lambourne and told me to stay there. You took my son away from me and wouldn't listen when I told you how much I missed him, and how lonely I was. You never came home, and if you did you had people with you and I felt like a housekeeper, not a wife. You hardly seemed to know I was alive over the last couple of years. Well, all that has to change. From now on, I want to share everything with you—not just your bed, Oliver. I want to work with you, and talk your problems out with you, see you every day, not once in a blue moon. That is the sort of marriage I want. An equal partnership.'

Oliver was staring at her now, his eyes shadowy, his face a mask she could not read. When she stopped talking, he didn't say anything for a full moment, and Francesca wondered desperately what he was thinking. Had he understood, at last, what she wanted? Why she had left him and come to London?

At last he said quietly, 'You've changed so much, Fran, don't you realise that? It's making my head spin. You were a shy, quiet, gentle girl when I married you, and before Jon was born you were a passionate woman in my bed, but after Jon was born you were so absorbed in him. You were a loving mother, I'm not saying you shouldn't have been—but you never seemed to have time for me then. All you cared about was the baby. When you came to bed you were usually too tired to make love, and you were preoccupied all day. Once Jon was on his feet, I thought we'd come closer together again, and we did, for a while, then you started talking about having another baby, and I knew that if we did it would happen all over again. Instead of you being mine, you would be theirs, you would belong to our children, not me, so I hoped we wouldn't have another baby. And then that made you unhappy, and I felt guilty, so I tried to give you a baby, but I couldn't.'

She stared at him blankly, stunned by all this, and Oliver gave her a sombre look, winnowing her long, pale hair with his fingers, watching the silvery fall of it against her skin, his eyes half closed.

'Women have no idea how that makes a man feel. It cut me in half; it made me miserable and angry. When you started talking about seeing a doctor to find out what was wrong, that made it worse, because I was afraid that if I did it might turn out that I was——' He broke off, his eyes shutting. 'Impotent,' he muttered thickly, and grimaced. 'The very word makes me ill. I got more and more obsessed with it, and in the end I stopped coming home because when I went to bed with you one day I was afraid I wouldn't even be able to make love to you, let alone give you a child.'

Francesca took a deep, shaky breath. 'That's why you came home so rarely?'

He nodded without looking at her.

'Why didn't you tell me?' She looked back over the years, appalled at realising how unhappy he must have been all that time. She had seen him withdraw, harden, grow cold to her, and had utterly misunderstood.

'I couldn't! The very thought of telling you terrified me. I was bitterly ashamed, Fran.' He leant his head on her shoulder, his skin burning against hers, shuddering physically like a frightened horse, and she stroked his hair, murmuring comfort to him, as she would to Jon.

'Darling, never mind, shh...there's nothing to be ashamed about...it's all right.'

The violent trembling stopped and he lay still, turning his face into her throat. Francesca quietly said, 'If I'd known, Oliver, I could have helped you, we wouldn't have drifted apart like this... I wouldn't be surprised to find out that there was nothing wrong with you at all, no earthly reason why you shouldn't father another child. It was probably all in your mind. It was your jealousy over Jon and your guilt and fear of having another baby that was the problem, nothing physical, and what you needed was to talk about it, bring it out into the open. If you had, the problem would have vanished.'

'Easier said than done,' he muttered without looking at her. 'It took a lot for me to tell you now. I couldn't have done it two years ago.'

She ruefully smiled to herself. 'Before I left you, you mean?'

He straightened and stood up, walking over to the window to look out, raking back his thick black hair with a hand that wasn't quite steady.

'Yes, you've cut the ground from under my feet,' he curtly admitted with his back to her. 'I can't lose

you, Fran. Come back to me. Let's start again, with
this real partnership you've been talking about—
I'm beginning to realise that that was the answer
all along, for you to come up to London, work with
me, share every day with me.'

'And no more babies?' she asked thoughtfully,
watching the line of his back, the clenched hands
at his side.

'An equal working partnership, you said,' he reminded. 'That is what you want, isn't it?'

'Yes,' she said, and decided it wasn't the time to
tell him her dream of having at least one other baby
in due course. That could come later.

'Then you will come back to me?' Oliver said,
turning to stare across the room at her.

'Give me a little breathing space,' she said,
smiling at him. 'We have plenty of time, Oliver. We
aren't in a hurry.'

'I am,' he said grimly. 'I want——'

The door was flung open before he could finish
that sentence, and they both jumped, looking round
at Matt staggering into the room under a pile of
modems and keyboards. He stared at them over
what he carried, said uneasily, 'Oh, hi!' then dived
towards the door to his workroom.

Francesca got up. 'I'd better go and help him.'

Oliver caught her arm. 'Don't keep me waiting
too long; my patience may run out!'

She smiled unsteadily at him and he stared down
at her mouth, the sound of his breathing audible,
the way he was watching her making her head swim,
then there was a crash from the workroom and the
sound of Matt swearing, and Francesca groaned.

'I must go...' She ran and Oliver stood there for a few seconds, then left too, the door slamming behind him. In the workroom she found Matt on his knees gingerly picking up and inspecting what he had dropped.

'Anything broken?' she asked, kneeling beside him to help.

He shook his head. 'Don't think so.' They got to their feet and piled everything on his workbench in a space Matt cleared among the usual clutter of electronic gadgets and parts. 'Oliver in a temper?' he asked, sitting down on his chair and picking up an eye glass so that he could inspect the wiring on a modem.

'No, not this time.'

'Was he complaining because we fixed an appointment for Garth Abbey to see Porta?'

'He started out by complaining about it, but I don't think he really minds.'

Matt looked relieved. 'Oh, well, thank the lord for that! It makes me nervous having Oliver breathing fire behind me all the time.' He glanced up at her, grimacing. 'But I'm going to have my work cut out getting Porta running perfectly by Friday, let me tell you!'

'You'll manage it with one hand tied behind your back,' she said, and Matt looked flattered, grinning.

'Thanks for the vote of confidence, but I shall need both hands, so I won't be tying one behind my back!'

She laughed at his joke dutifully, brought him coffee, then left him to his work while she got on with her own. Over the next few days Matt worked at an even more hectic pace than usual. He was always there when she arrived in the morning, he was always at his workbench when she left in the evening, and she strongly suspected that if she had returned in the middle of the night she would have found him there.

During the rest of that week she did not see much of Oliver, either, because he had to fly to Brussels on business. At least this time he had not taken Janice with him. Francesca met her from time to time, in corridors, or lifts, and they gave each other frozen glances, but Janice was being very careful at the moment. She had stopped making those barbed insinuations. Had Oliver said something to her? Francesca wondered, and then couldn't help wondering what had really happened between Oliver and Janice.

She had been half joking when she'd told him she wanted him to fire Janice, but part of her felt that her marriage would never be safe while the redhead was around. Janice wanted Oliver, too. Her jealous eyes admitted as much, silently, whenever she looked at Francesca.

Oliver had sworn that he hadn't had an affair with her, but had he been lying? Had he now told Janice the affair was over, for the time being at least?

Francesca wished she could be sure of him, but Oliver was secretive—look at the way he had hidden from her his feelings about having another baby. She had had no idea what was going on inside his head all these years and, although he had told her about that now, what else had he hidden from her?

If he had had an affair with his secretary, she wanted to know about it, even if it was over. He might not ever intend to resume his affair with Janice, but if she was still working for him Janice was the type to keep putting temptation his way. Would she accept the end of their affair?

Whatever the truth, Francesca felt she had to know all of it before she could feel able to trust Oliver completely.

He flew back on the Friday morning, determined to be present when Mr Abbey arrived. He came straight to Matt's workroom and found him hunched over his machine, still making tiny adjustments, running tests. Francesca heard Oliver's voice as she came back from having coffee with several of the other girls. Her heart turned over, making her feel quite sick, and she took several deep breaths before she went into the other room.

He straightened to look round at her, looking taller than ever, his black hair smoothed down, his cashmere overcoat over his arm and his pinstriped suit very elegant.

'Hello,' she said shyly, and he smiled, the grey eyes warm.

'Hello.'

Matt went on working, quite unaware of the atmosphere in the room, the way the other two were looking at each other.

The phone rang in her office, and Francesca fled to answer it, her smile going as she recognised Janice's high-pitched voice.

'Is Oliver there?' Janice asked peremptorily. 'Reception told me he was in the building and he isn't here; is he there?'

'Yes, I'll get him,' Francesca said coldly, put down the phone and went to find Oliver. He gave her a quick glance as she said Janice wanted him, then went through to her office. She did not follow; she stayed with Matt, trying hard not to listen to Oliver's voice in the other room.

He came to the door a moment later, said curtly, 'I've got to go. I'll be back when Abbey arrives.'

Francesca did not look at him; neither did Matt, who barely knew he was there. After waiting briefly, Oliver strode out.

Mr Abbey arrived ten minutes later; they rang from reception to tell Francesca, saying that they hadn't been able to get through to Oliver's office yet; he had had an urgent call from Hong Kong and they dared not interrupt.

'I'll come down and get Mr Abbey,' Francesca said. 'Leave it with me.'

She went down, and found Mr Abbey waiting. He smiled in his cherubic way when he recognised her, offering his hand. 'Mrs Ransom, this is a pleasure! How are you?'

He chatted all the way up to Matt's floor, an easy flow of small talk she had no difficulty answering. She escorted him to Matt's workroom, offered to make him coffee, took in two cups which both men absently put down on a table before going back to their absorbed discussion of the new portable computer. Francesca watched them wryly, then hurried back to her own office and tried to ring Oliver, but his line was still engaged. She then rang Janice, but although that phone rang nobody picked it up. Francesca hesitated, frowning. Oliver would be furious if he was not told at once that Mr Abbey was in the building. She had to make sure he knew. She would have to go to his office and tell him in person.

She went in to tell Matt where she was going, but he merely nodded and waved her away, so she rushed along the corridor to take the stairs, running all the way.

Janice was not in her outer office, which explained why she had not answered her phone; she must be having a coffee-break.

Francesca opened the door into Oliver's office, meaning to mouth her message to him silently if he was still talking on the phone.

He wasn't, though, and she froze on the spot, a jagged pain tearing through her as she stared across the room. Oliver was not talking on the phone. Janice was not having coffee. She was sitting on Oliver's lap, her arms around his neck, kissing him passionately.

CHAPTER EIGHT

FRANCESCA must have made a sound, a gasp perhaps, a half-stifled cry of jealousy and pain, although she wasn't aware of moving or reacting in any way.

All the same, Oliver must have heard her, because he suddenly put his hands over Janice's wrists and pulled her arms down, pushing her away from him.

His head lifted, was thrown back, as if to escape the mouth still hunting for his own; he flashed a glance towards the door. Janice was laughing carelessly, snuggling into him, but over her vibrant red head he stared across the room at the white-faced woman in the doorway. His face turned a dark, startled red; he looked guilty, disturbed, as well he might. He had been caught red-handed. He couldn't lie his way out of this.

Pulling herself together, Francesca said huskily, 'Mr Abbey is here.' She didn't wait for Oliver to respond; she didn't want to hear what he had to say. She had seen enough to be utterly certain now. Oliver was not lying to her again.

'Francesca!' he said in a deep, harsh voice as she turned on her heel, but she ignored him and closed the door carefully behind her before she went back to Matt's workroom.

It was foolish to feel so shaken and betrayed. She had suspected all along, hadn't she? She had begun to wonder months ago, puzzled by Oliver's lack of interest in her, by his long absences and his cold remoteness, picking up the malice and dislike in Janice's voice whenever they spoke on the telephone. It had all pointed to one answer—that Oliver was having an affair with his secretary—and everyone had been dropping hints since she started work here. Matt had betrayed his suspicions by his unhappy expression every time the subject of Janice came up, Oliver lied but always looked so self-conscious when they talked about his secretary, and Janice herself, of course, had wanted her to know, had practically thrust the truth at her. It was in Janice's interest for the affair to become public knowledge. Janice was a clever, ambitious girl; she wanted more than the role of Oliver's mistress, she wanted to be his wife. Well, maybe she would get what she wanted now.

Francesca paused outside Matt's door, taking a deep breath and fighting for control of her expression. It wasn't until she was sure she looked perfectly normal that she opened the door and joined the two men.

Mr Abbcy looked up, smiled. 'Ah, Mrs Ransom! This is a very impressive machine Mr Keilner has here! I'm very stuck by the way it runs, but the proof of it is going to be whether it is as easily portable as he claims.'

She managed a bright smile in reply and went over to the workbench, said, 'May I?' to Matt, who grinned back at her, then sat down and began to get out of the program they had been running. Once that was done, she withdrew the disk they had been working on, switched off the computer, unplugged it, coiled the lead into the base of the VDU, slid the carrying box over the screen, fitted the keyboard into a side pocket, locked the entire thing in place, lifted the handle and stood up. She walked to the door carrying the computer in its box while Mr Abbey and Matt watched her.

At the door, she turned. 'Notice, it took me less than two minutes to get this far from actually being in the process of operating the computer,' she said to Mr Abbey, who nodded, then Francesca walked calmly back to him, and handed him the box to demonstrate how light it was.

He took it and weighed it in one hand, nodding. 'Amazing. But you would need a power source to operate it?'

'Or you can switch over to the rechargeable batteries. They run forever if you keep them topped up by plugging them into the mains for a few hours between use.'

The door opened abruptly and Oliver strode in, his features taut and grim, his eyes skimming the room in search of her. She fought to keep control of her face and voice, and managed to win.

'Here's my husband,' she said coolly to Mr Abbey, who went forward to meet Oliver, one hand outstretched in greeting, while he still carried the computer in the other hand.

'This is one hell of a toy you have here!' he informed Oliver, shaking hands and quite unaware of the other man's scarcely veiled impatience at having to be polite to him.

'Oh, thank you, yes, isn't it?' Oliver said, shooting a sideways look at Francesca, his black lashes half cloaking his grey eyes.

'But it isn't a toy,' Francesca said quickly, and Mr Abbey turned back to her, that cherubic look on his face again.

'Well, now, I don't see many business men travelling the world with one of these in their luggage, or taking along their secretary to operate the thing, and if we can't sell it in sufficient numbers to the business community who do we sell it to, except as a toy?'

'Business men will carry it,' Francesca insisted. 'It will be invaluable to them, both to key in information they need to record, which can later be transferred to the office computer, on disk—and so that while they are away they can send material directly to their office computer, via a telephone link. Let us show you . . .'

She politely relieved him of the prototype and Matt began to demonstrate that aspect of Porta. Oliver stood slightly behind Francesca, his shoulder almost touching her, and she was very aware of vibrations coming from him. He might want to sell the new portable to Mr Abbey, but at the moment he was finding it hard to concentrate. Frustration and tension came from him in waves, and Francesca decided to get away as soon as possible before she had the unavoidable clash with him.

'Porta may be small and lightweight, but she has immense capacity,' said Matt happily, enjoying

himself. His latest project was always the best thing
he had ever done, and for the moment Porta was
his dream come true. His eyes shone and whenever
he met Francesca's eyes he smiled, his face radiant.
He was delighted with Mr Abbey's reaction, even
though the other man was looking hard for some
defect in the machine. Matt didn't mind that. Porta
was being tested and, if Mr Abbey did find some
flaw in her, Matt would be only too happy to work
like a slave until he had corrected the error.

Mr Abbey didn't forget Francesca; half his quite
searching questions were directed her way and she
usually managed to answer him, even if at times
she had to look at Matt enquiringly to make sure
she was giving the right answer.

'You really know your stuff, Mrs Ransom,' Mr
Abbey congratulated her at one point. 'You three
make a good team.'

A few hours ago, that would have been music to
her ears. Now she had difficulty smiling.

Oliver was watching her, so she held back the
sigh threatening to escape. She was not going to
give him the satisfaction of knowing how much he
had hurt her. Matt was explaining another special
feature of Porta; Mr Abbey was bending beside
him, listening intently. Oliver caught her arm and
Francesca stiffened, shooting him a contemptuous
look, silently trying to free herself without at-
tracting Mr Abbey's attention.

Oliver jerked his head towards the door,
mouthing, 'Come outside!'

She shook her head and managed to pull free.
At once she moved further away, so that she was

now within Mr Abbey's eyeline, knowing that Oliver wouldn't hassle her if the other man could see what was going on.

Oliver's brows met, black and heavy above his narrowed grey eyes, but he made no further attempt to get her on her own. After a moment, he said, 'Mr Abbey, will you be free to lunch with me today?'

'That would have been delightful! Unfortunately, I have another appointment, but I hope we can get together for lunch some other day before I go back to the States?' Mr Abbey looked at his watch. 'In fact, I'm grateful you reminded me . . . I have to leave very soon or I shall be late. Mr Ransom, can we get down to facts and figures now? I've seen enough of what Porta can do to be sure it is what we've been looking for . . . if the price is right, of course! The product has to sell to the public at a price they feel comfortable with! Pitch it too high and however marvellous it may be, they won't buy—but I'm preaching to the converted, I'm sure.' He smiled, that cherubic charm masking a shrewd mind, and Oliver warily smiled back, undeceived by the other's wide eyes and look of innocence.

'Come along to my office,' invited Oliver. 'We can get down to details in comfort.'

'Thank you.' Mr Abbey courteously shook hands with Francesca and then with Matt, thanking them both for their time and trouble, then followed Oliver out of the room.

'Nice guy,' Matt said cheerfully. 'He really knows his markets, too; he was telling me some fascinating stuff while you were gone. The Japanese are pretty advanced in my field; we'll be lucky if we sell Porta to that firm. Great opportunity for us!' He swung back along his workbench and began operating Porta again, whistling through his teeth.

Francesca stared out of the window, seeing that the sky had turned grey and it looked as if it might rain. The weather matched her mood; a bleak weariness seemed to have swept down over her. Any minute now Oliver might come back, and she couldn't stand the thought of having to listen to him lie. She despised him; her heart ached.

'Matt, can I have the rest of the day off?' she asked abruptly, and he swung round to stare at her, his expression a mixture of concern and surprise.

'Of course you can—is something wrong? Aren't you feeling well, Fran?' He got up and she almost burst into tears at his gentleness; her lip trembled and Matt looked horrified. 'Fran! Good heavens, what is it?' He put his arms around her and she leaned on him for a second or two, tempted to cling, to confide, then felt Matt rest his cheek on her hair, his arms tightening.

'Darling Fran,' he said huskily, and she turned rigid, her hidden face stricken. She had never meant to hurt Matt, to encourage him to grow too fond of her, but for days she had secretly been aware that his friendship was becoming something else, and she was ashamed. She should have made it crystal-clear that she didn't feel anything but a sisterly affection for him. She had been hoping it would never need to be said, but the moment she had hoped to avoid was here, and what on earth was she going to do?

Her brain raced, looking for a way out that would save Matt's face, somehow make it possible for them to go on being friends.

'Tell me what's wrong,' Matt whispered, his lips on her hair.

She was already on the verge of tears; she let them come, sobbing audibly. 'Oh, Matt...it's Oliver...'

'What has he done to you?' Matt growled, sounding very aggressive.

'I just wish I didn't love him so much,' she whispered, and felt Matt tighten. He stood still and she gave another little sob. 'I can't help being jealous over Janice...they're having an affair, I know they are, but I can't stop loving him just like that...you can't shut love off like a tap. Well, I can't. I'm a one-man woman, even if at the moment I'd like to kill Oliver.'

Matt still had an arm around her, but he was no longer kissing her hair, or holding her quite so tightly.

'He isn't worth crying over, he's a selfish bastard,' he muttered thickly, then pretended to cough to clear his throat, and in doing so let go of Francesca, who hunted for a handkerchief, wiped her eyes, blew her nose, her body half turned away from Matt so that he could not see her face. She could not see his, either, which gave them both time to don protective expressions.

'I thought I'd drive to Jon's school this weekend,' she said quietly, still not looking at Matt. 'I can visit Jon, take him out for a drive and some lunch.

But don't tell Oliver, will you? He mentioned
something about visiting Jon, and I don't want to
find myself forced into a threesome. I'll make sure
I get there really early, then I can drive off with
Jon before Oliver can catch up with us. Oliver can
see him some other time. I want Jon to myself for
a few hours. He may be worried about what's happening at home; you never know what boys are
thinking. If he sees me, it will reassure him. Promise
me you won't breathe a word, Matt.'

'I won't,' he said flatly. 'You can trust me.'

She smiled at him then, sadness in her eyes as
well as affection. 'I do, Matt, you know that.'

She should have been more careful with him, kept
a distance between them. It had been selfish and
thoughtless of her to let Matt's feelings change
without doing anything about it.

She couldn't say it was a complete surprise; she
had begun to sense that he was looking at her in a
new way. He hadn't even given her a second look
before. Oh, he had liked her, maybe Oliver was right
about a hidden attraction—Oliver knew Matt far
better than she did, and Oliver was a man, he might
well pick up such secret feelings in another man!
But it wasn't until he thought she had left Oliver
for good, and was available, that Matt really felt
free to let himself be attracted to her. He was that
sort of man; he had simple, traditional attitudes,
and Francesca admired them in him. Matt was the
faithful type; he had a strong code of morality. He
wouldn't betray a friend by trying to steal his wife,
any more than he would betray his wife with other
women.

A pity Oliver was not more like Matt!

'I'll tell Oliver you asked for the day off to buy some clothes,' Matt said.

'Good idea! That will put him off the scent for a while, anyway.'

'But you'd better go now before he comes looking for you!' Matt sounded more like himself. He would soon get over her; his feelings had not had time to put down deep roots and, as Matt did not suppose she had any suspicions, he would not have to feel guilty or self-conscious in her presence. He could revert back to his old cheerful, friendly self— as a disguise at first, and then quite naturally when the pretence became the reality.

'See you on Monday,' she said, and hurried away. She went back to her flat to pack a case. She was about to leave when the phone rang. She hesitated, staring at it, then decided it would be wiser to answer it so that Oliver would believe she was still in London.

'Hello?' she asked huskily.

'Francesca, we are going to talk, whether you like it or not,' Oliver's deep, insistent voice said.

'Leave me alone!' she whispered, tears at once pricking her eyes at the mere sound of his voice. She ran a hand over her lids angrily; she was not going to cry over him. Matt had been right—Oliver wasn't worth it.

'You know I'm not going to do that,' he drawled, and of course she did know. Oliver had too much to lose if she left him. He would fight like a trapped tiger to hold on to his company.

'I don't want to talk to you. You lied to me!'

'No, Fran! I know what it looked like, but you're wrong! I tried to tell you at the office, but you wouldn't listen. You jumped to the wrong conclusions. I wasn't kissing Janice...'

Francesca laughed contemptuously. 'I must see an optician, then, because I sure as hell saw you kissing her!'

'No!' he said with impatience. 'Just listen to me...look, we have to see each other. I'm tied up all day, but I'm free this evening...have dinner with me.' He was so sure she would; his insolence made her eyes flash. He must despise her to think she would be such a pushover!

She had seen him with Janice on his lap, her arms around his neck. She had seen them kiss—and yet Oliver still thought he could persuade her she was wrong? He must think her an utter fool. Her face burned with humiliation.

'I'll pick you up at seven,' he said with casual arrogance, and she seethed. The very sound of his voice made her want to throw things.

'I don't want to see you!' she hissed. 'I won't open the door!'

Oliver coolly said, 'See you then,' and put the phone down. She flung down her own receiver and glared at it, shaking with anger. That was what he thought! How dared he be so damn sure of himself? Or so insultingly sure of her? Well, he was going to learn different.

She picked up her case and headed for the door and her car. When Oliver arrived at seven tonight to pick her up he could ring the doorbell until hell froze over. She wasn't going to be there. She was putting time and distance between herself and Oliver. That would give her time to work out what she really wanted to do, how she was going to treat Oliver in future.

Jon's school was in Yorkshire. It would take her hours to drive up there, and she would need a short rest en route, so she decided to stop for lunch at a country pub on the way.

She made a simple meal: a stick of French bread, a selection of cheeses, and a plate of mixed salad. With that she just drank mineral water, followed by one cup of coffee.

The break at least made the journey seem shorter, but as she drove on northwards the weather worsened and with faint anxiety she watched the leaden sky sagging low over the flat Midlands through which she passed. It was very cold, too. She was wearing a sheepskin driving jacket which kept her warm enough, but she felt the chill of the winter wind on her face with the window open, so she closed it and turned up the heating in the car.

In London it was easy to forget the rigours of winter, but it was almost December and those heavy grey clouds might herald snow. She glanced at her watch, frowning. The further north she went, the colder it would probably be—and the likelier the chance of snow. Would she reach her destination before the first flakes fell?

It had not occurred to her that snow might already be falling in the north, but as she reached the top of a very steep hill she caught a glimpse of the landscape spread below her, stretching away into Yorkshire, and the entire countryside was white.

Hills, moors, dales, all cloaked in snow; trees dressed with it, as if for Christmas, bushes buried in it, and, like the cars and houses, disguised by it into strange, bewildering shapes. Francesca did not recognise the landscape under the snow, and stared, frowning. The faint rays of the dying afternoon sun glittered on silvery branches, icy windows, lakes and streams rapidly freezing over.

It would grow even colder as night fell and the light of the sun vanished. The roads would ice up; driving would become dangerous and she hadn't yet reached the village where she had meant to stay. She had rung to book a room before she packed, and hadn't had any problems because at this time of year few people were on the road or visiting the village. In summer, it was different, because this was an area of great natural beauty and attracted many tourists in the season.

When she and Oliver had brought Jon up here to see the school during the summer holidays they had all stayed at a delightful country hotel; a seventeenth-century coaching inn which had been expanded with a new, modern building at the rear of the old one, but designed in a careful period style to match the rest.

It was the only place to stay within easy driving distance of the school, but the village, like the school itself, was off the main road, buried in the countryside, and Francesca had an uneasy feeling that by the time she reached the turning off the motorway it would be dark and the roads would be glassy with ice.

Perhaps she should turn off now, find somewhere else to stay tonight, and see how the weather looked tomorrow morning?

She slowed, hesitating. She hadn't let Jon know she was coming, although she had rung the school and warned them that she would try to get up to see Jon that weekend. She could still change her mind—but she wanted to see her son. She missed him; she had to be sure he was OK. She was going on, however bad the weather. Only another hour and she would be safely at the village inn.

But an hour later she was hunched over the driving wheel, peering rather helplessly through whirling snowflakes at a strange, white landscape, lost on roads she could not recognise or find on her map. She kept catching a glimpse of lights somewhere ahead, but the twists and turns of the narrow lanes never seemed to lead to any houses, and she was getting frightened. Her fuel was low; she hadn't found a garage for a long time and she was afraid she would run out before she reached the village where she would be staying.

It couldn't be far now, surely? She swung round a blind corner and almost ran smack into a van coming down hill towards her. The van veered sideways to avoid her, horn blaring, the lights almost dazzling her.

Francesca took avoiding action, too, jamming on her brakes. The car skidded all over the road but eventually stopped. She switched off the engine and leaned on her wheel, pale and shaky. In her driving mirror she saw the van's tail-lights disappear on

down the hill. Silence descended; the snow blew
wildly against her windscreen, blanketing it.

She waited a minute to get her nerve back, then
switched on the ignition. The engine coughed
weakly, but the car did not start.

'Oh, no!' she muttered, trying again, her foot on
the accelerator to catch the slightest burst of life.
Another feeble spluttering; she desperately tried to
nurse it into real power, but it died and after that
she couldn't even get a splutter out of it. The car
wasn't going anywhere. Neither was she.

She was stranded here, in a snowstorm, on a
lonely, unfamiliar road, with no idea where she was
or how far it was to the nearest house.

She sat with her hands on the steering wheel,
listening, staring through the blinding snow. What
on earth was she going to do?

Stay here and freeze to death? Get out and try
to find the village? You could die of exposure
walking across unknown countryside in weather like
this; it would be safer to stay in the car. A van had
just driven past. Another car might come along any
minute, and meanwhile she would just have to make
herself as warm and comfortable as she could.

She had slung her case into the back of the car;
she leaned over and opened it, found several
sweaters, a pair of jeans, some woollen socks.

She put them all on and crammed herself back
into her sheepskin, which then only just managed
to button up. There was a tartan travelling rug
folded up under the back seat. She drew that up to
her chin and huddled down under it, half hysterical
at the thought of how she must look. But she was

warm! Who cared how she looked? Nobody who mattered was going to see her.

She stared out into the flying snow until her eyes glazed and her lids felt heavy. They slowly closed and she drifted into a half sleep, then woke with a jerk of shock.

She mustn't sleep. She had to stay awake and alert so that if a car came along she could flag it down. But that was easier said than done; the warmth and silence combined with her weariness after the long car journey made sleep dangerously attractive. She kept drifting off into a doze, then snapping awake, but it was a losing battle; finally her head slid sideways against the leather seat, and sleep won.

She slept so deeply that when another car came by she did not hear the muffled note of the engine. Nor did she hear the car skid to a halt, or the snow-blurred footsteps of the man walking back to peer in through her window.

He walked round the car and climbed in through the passenger door, closed it behind him and leaned over her to stare, carefully brushed a strand of blonde hair back so that he could see her face, then lifted the travelling rug and ran his eyes down over her sleeping body.

Francesca still didn't wake up. What finally got through to her sleep-drowned mind was the movements of his hands; they touched her throat, paused, stroked downwards. He watched her, a glitter in his eyes, smiling oddly, as if waiting for her to wake up. His hands crept up under her sweaters. His fingers were cold; her breasts were warm. She came back to consciousness like a salmon shooting up through icy water; gasping, shocked. Her eyes opened as wide as they could, to pierce the strange snowlit gloom in the car, and then she screamed.

CHAPTER NINE

'STOP screaming, you stupid woman! It's me!'

'I know that! Why else do you think I screamed?'
Fran said coldly. 'Just get your hands off me.'

'Why the hell should I?' Oliver snarled, glaring
at her, but his hands came out into the open where
she could see them. 'You're lucky I didn't slap you
awake.'

'I'd rather you had!'

She was glad to see that that really annoyed him.
He scowled at her. 'Don't press your luck! I'm so
angry with you I could hit you right here and now.
What in hell's name did you think you were doing?
Parking by the side of a road and then going to
sleep, leaving the doors unlocked! Haven't you any
common sense? You were lucky it was me who
found you first. It could have been someone
dangerous.'

'Wasn't it?'

The irony was wasted on him. 'Don't be stupid,
Fran!' he said, brushing her dry tone aside. 'And
another thing...what possessed you to drive up here
on a day when the weather forecast was for bliz-
zards and blocked roads in this area?'

'I didn't listen to the weather forecast, it never
occurred to me that it might snow this early in the
winter.' She looked at the swirling flakes still ob-
scuring the landscape, then frowned as something

else occurred to her. 'Come to that . . . what are you doing up here today? You were talking of having dinner in London tonight. What changed your mind?' Her blue eyes darkened with surprise and anger. 'Did Matt tell you?' She saw Oliver's eyes flicker slightly. 'He did, didn't he? How could he? He promised he wouldn't.'

'Matt didn't want to break his promise. He had to, for your sake.'

Francesca made a low, angry sound, her face scornful. 'Oh, yes, of course, it would be! Typical male thinking!'

'You ought to know Matt better.' Oliver's brows were a hard black line above his grey eyes. 'He was in my office talking about the Porta order, and I turned on the stock market report to listen to the latest share prices.'

She laughed shortly. 'What has that got to do with Matt breaking his promise to me?'

'I'll tell you, if you'll let me! We caught the tail end of the news, and that was how we heard about the blizzard conditions up here. I saw Matt's face, he went quite pale and was obviously very worried. He didn't say anything, but I've known him since we were at school, remember. I can almost read Matt's mind at times.'

'Do you think I was born yesterday?'

'Sometimes there's no other explanation for your crazy behaviour!'

'You expect me to believe that you read Matt's thoughts and guessed I had come up here? You've suddenly developed powers of telepathy?' Her biting tone made his mouth curl impatiently.

'I'm not claiming supernatural powers, just logic and a touch of what they call female intuition, although it can be just as easily experienced by men. I put two and two together, in other words—realised Jon's school was in the blizzard area, remembered that you had gone off without warning this morning and that we had talked about spending a weekend with Jon soon. All that—and Matt's face as he heard about the freak snowstorms around here—made me jump to a conclusion. I asked Matt outright—Has Francesca gone to visit Jon at school?—and he looked confused and mumbled that he didn't know what I meant, so I told him that if he didn't give me a straight answer to a straight question, and anything happened to you on your way up here, I'd cut him into tiny bits and feed him to the pigeons.'

'Oh, big man!' she coldly mocked, and Oliver gave her a menacing look meant to make her knees tremble. Francesca just stared back in defiance. 'So Matt caved in and told you?'

He grabbed hold of her and shook her. 'Will you stop talking to me like that? Matt was worried about you. So was I. Why do you think I drove up here like a crazy man, on roads like skating rinks at the end? I had visions of your car skidding, turning over in some ditch...and then I saw it parked at the side of the road. For one minute I thought you really had had a bad crash—until I saw you, then I parked, and came over to make sure you weren't injured.'

She gave him a bitter smile. 'And that's why you had your hands inside my sweater when I woke up, of course!'

Oliver's eyes glittered angrily. 'You don't seem to realise how stupid you've been! If it hadn't been me who had found you, you might well have woken up to find yourself in very dangerous company. I just wanted to show you what could have happened to you!'

She laughed scornfully, her face disbelieving. 'Oh, now you claim you were only teaching me a lesson?'

'And I hope you learnt it! Next time you find yourself alone on a lonely road, lock the car doors and don't fall asleep. You've been lucky.'

He was still gripping her shoulders, his fingers hurting. She struggled furiously, looking up at him with hatred. 'Lucky? To wake up and find you mauling me? Keep your attentions for Janice Sylvester. I don't want you anywhere near me!'

'Listen to me, Fran...' he began, his eyes wary, but she wasn't listening, never again.

'I don't want to know! I've heard enough of your lies to last me a lifetime. You don't pull the wool over my eyes again.'

'Fran...' he began again, and her temper boiled over; she hit him, as hard as she could.

She heard the deep, savage breath he took; saw his skin turn white with rage. She should have been scared by that, but instead she felt a queer stabbing triumph, because Oliver was no longer quite so much in control of himself, he wasn't Mr Invincible, Mr Superman any more—he was coming

down to her level, the human level, the place where
you could get hurt and hurt back.

She waited for him to explode in anger, thinking
for a second that he might even hit her back, but
instead he swooped like a hawk taking prey—his
mouth primitive, devouring, rending her, making
her shake with that secret beat of the blood which
was the bond between victim and predator. His
mouth was hot, it melted her flesh; she tried desperately to hold out, but it was not really Oliver
she was fighting, it was her own desire for the silken
sweetness of their bodies twisting in the dark, the
intensity of that moment when she reached the peak
of pleasure and fell downwards, moaning, crying
out in agonised happiness. She despised herself. She
had summoned all her reason, all her intelligence;
and Oliver was bypassing them to speak to her
body.

He kissed her yielding mouth softly. 'Fran, you'll
listen now, won't you?' he said, his voice thick with
satisfaction.

She had forgotten everything else for a moment,
but Oliver hadn't. She had gone crazy, but he hadn't
lost his head at all. He had just been putting her
into the right mood to listen to more of his plausible lies. Well, she wasn't going to listen to them!
He need not think he had won!

She brought her teeth together on his lower lip
and Oliver almost went through the roof of the car.

'You little bitch!' he swore violently. 'What the
hell did you do that for?' He sat up, letting go of
her, his face incredulous, dark with angry blood.
He ran a fingertip over the graze on his lip and then

peered at his finger through the gloom in the car. 'It's bleeding!' he said in shock.

Francesca opened the door and dived out, ran towards his car. Snow blew around her, her feet skidded and slid. The blizzard was worsening; the wind was stronger, the snow thicker. She heard Oliver shouting behind her; she ignored him, climbing in behind the wheel of his car. He had left the car-keys in the ignition; she removed them and pushed them into her pocket just as Oliver pulled the driver's door open again.

'Get out of there!'

She shook her head, and when he tried to drag her out she clung on to the steering wheel, her face stubborn. Oliver suddenly let go of her, his eyes on the ignition switch.

'Where are my keys? What the hell do you think you're playing at?'

'You can have them back when you've brought my luggage over here and locked up my car. We'll swap car keys and you can drive me on to the hotel.'

He stared, eyes hard, then slammed the door shut, turned on his heel and strode back to her car. Francesca sighed in exhausted relief and put her head down on the steering wheel. She thought longingly of a warm hotel: hot drinks, food, a comfortable bed.

She heard Oliver slinging her case into the car, he opened the driver's door again, held out her car keys. 'Move over!' he barked as she silently exchanged them for his own keys, and Francesca was only too happy to obey.

Oliver dropped the tartan rug into her lap before he climbed behind the steering wheel. Francesca snuggled down into the warm folds and closed her eyes, glad to be able to leave the driving to him under these arctic conditions. The car slowly bumped along, she was aware of Oliver tensely concentrating beside her, leaning forward to watch the road ahead for warning headlights coming towards them. Visibility was very low and she knew it couldn't be any fun for him, but she felt safer with Oliver at the wheel. He was a very good driver; she knew she wasn't at all bad herself, but Oliver had the edge on her. His reflexes were faster, and he had nerves of steel.

She yawned, and Oliver glanced drily down at her. 'Comfortable?'

'Yes, thanks,' she said. 'All I need now is a stiff drink to help me get off to sleep.'

Oliver leaned forward and opened the glove compartment; a small light illuminated the inside. 'Help yourself,' he said, as she sat forward to stare at the small hip-flask.

'What is it?' She opened the flask and sniffed uncertainly. She didn't drink much and wasn't sure about the contents.

'Brandy.' Oliver swore as headlights blazed into their eyes. The car skidded sideways and almost went into a stone wall as a lorry passed them at a dangerous speed. Oliver shouted an insult after the driver, and Francesca took a dubious taste of the brandy, grimacing.

'Do you want some?' she asked Oliver, who raised his brows.

'Are you kidding? I need all my wits about me to cope with this driving. I'm not drinking until I get to the hotel.'

Francesca took another sip of brandy; it was warm and slid smoothly down her throat, leaving her feeling even more relaxed and comfortable. She closed her eyes and drank a little more. Oliver's car was far more luxurious than her own, of course. The leather had an opulent smell; the seat was so deeply upholstered that she was sinking into it. The heating worked better, too. She drifted softly into a doze, her head sinking sideways until it came to rest on something firm and warm.

When she woke up the car had stopped moving, the engine was switched off; she dazedly looked around and Oliver had gone. She was alone.

She rubbed a small circle on the windscreen to peer out, and saw lights; they were parked beside a building and she saw a sign swinging in the wind, but driving snow had blanked out whatever was painted on it. It looked like a pub, judging by the leaded windows and a cosy look about the place. It wasn't the hotel she had been making for, she was certain of that.

She heard footsteps, the door opened and Oliver looked in at her. 'Oh, you're awake! I didn't want to disturb you if they didn't have any rooms, but we're in luck. Out you get. I'll bring the luggage.'

Francesca got out of the car just as the icy wind launched a new attack. Bent almost double, she ran to the lighted doorway she could just see, her face lashed by stinging needles of snow, her teeth aching from the cold. She dashed inside and sank down, panting, on an old oak bench whose leather-covered cushions were faded and threadbare. A few men sat around an old-fashioned bar, pints of beer in their fists. They stared stolidly at her in the heavy silence.

A middle-aged woman in a clean white apron came from some inner room and gave her a polite smile. 'Good evening, Mrs Ransom. I'm Mrs White, the landlady here. No night for travelling, is it?' She sounded as if she did not approve of people travelling anyway, and Francesca smiled back rather stiffly and explained.

'We were visiting our son, he is at boarding-school near here...'

'So your husband said. Well, we don't usually take overnight guests, this is just a pub, you know, not a hotel, but on a night like this I wouldn't turn a dog away.'

Francesca wasn't sure if that was a joke; she compromised with a weak smile. 'You're very kind, thank you...'

Mrs White did not smile back. She looked as if she considered more than the occasional smile rather frivolous. She was a heavy, angular woman with stern eyes and a rather grim mouth. Francesca found her distinctly nerve-racking.

'You'll want to go straight up to your room,' she said, as Oliver appeared, carrying Francesca's case, and there was a definite softening in her manner now that he was there. Mrs White was, it seemed, a man's woman!

'Come this way,' she said, leading them out of the bar and up some dark and winding stairs.

'There's plenty of hot water for that bath you said you were wanting, Mr Ransom, and I can have a good home-cooked meal on the table whenever you're ready for it.' She threw Francesca a sideways look of faint disapproval. 'Nothing grand, mind— just plain home cooking: a steak and kidney pudding with vegetables, and then there's baked apples to follow.'

'Stuffed with dried fruit and brown sugar?' Oliver asked with what Francesca considered to be a greedy note in his voice.

'Oh, aye,' Mrs White said, opening a door on the landing at the top of the stairs. 'And I serve my apples with whipped cream.' She had warmed up considerably by now; her eyes approved of Oliver, who put on the hungriest look he knew.

'I can't wait,' he said, and Mrs White beamed at him.

'Have your bath first, and come down in an hour.'

She vanished back down the stairs while Francesca was looking blankly around the large, gloomily furnished room. It held a Victorian bed of enormous proportions with a carved wooden bedhead and bulbous legs. The red velvet cover on the bed matched the curtains at the high windows. The room was chilly, but Oliver was kneeling at a vast hearth, lighting a carefully laid fire.

'Is this my room or yours?' Francesca asked as a flame shot up through the elegant pyramid of pine cones balanced on logs underpinned by a nest of coals.

'I hope this chimney doesn't smoke. She swore it didn't,' said Oliver, admiring his work with his head to one side.

'Oliver! Whose room is this?' Francesca asked, a horrible suspicion gnawing at her insides.

'There is only one guest room in the place,' Oliver said casually, getting to his feet.

'I don't believe you! I'm going down to ask that woman for another room,' Francesca said, turning to the door.

'I wouldn't,' said Oliver.

'I'm sure you wouldn't!' she seethed, eyeing him with intense dislike.

'She only gave us this room because I assured her we were married. She told me she didn't approve of casual sex.'

Francesca gave him a freezing glance. 'Nor do I, which is why I refuse to share a room with you!'

'If you go down and tell her we're not the respectably conventional couple I've been at great pains to make her think we are, she'll turn us both out into the snow!'

The fire was leaping up the chimney now; the blaze and heat reached her and made her aware of the coldness in her very bones. She was tired; Oliver was tired.

'And I'm starving,' Oliver said wistfully. 'I refuse to be cheated of that steak and kidney pudding, or the delicious baked apples with cream.'

'I'm not sleeping with you!' Francesca said bitterly, staring at the vastness of the velvet-draped bed. It looked so invitingly comfortable; she was sure it was a feather bed and the thought of sinking into it and going to sleep in a firelit room was too tempting to resist.

'I'll make myself a bed by the fire,' Oliver said, and began to undo his shirt.

'What do you think you're doing?' She backed, her body tense, but he gave her a mocking glance from under his lashes, smiling, as he pulled off his jacket and then his shirt.

'I'm going to be first in that hot bath!' He vanished through a far door and she heard the sound of water running, then Oliver came back, his lean body naked except for a pair of blue briefs. She swallowed, her mouth dry, hurriedly looking away as he unlocked the small travelling case which was all he had brought with him. He took out an immaculately ironed white shirt and hung it in the great carved oak wardrobe which matched the bed. Then he fished out a clean pair of socks and some clean underpants.

Francesca turned her back on him and began to unpack her own things, her pulses beating a violent tattoo every time he moved. 'Don't take all the hot water!' she muttered crossly as he came far too close, sending shivers down her back as she involuntarily caught sight of his bare thigh, the black hairs roughening his long legs.

'We used to share our baths,' drawled Oliver in a tone of nostalgia.

She pretended not to hear him, but she remembered it and her heart twisted in pain. They had been so much in love in those first years of their marriage. They had rarely been apart: had worked together, lived together, slept together.

'We could share this one,' Oliver tempted.

She went on hanging clothes up, her back to him, and after a moment the bathroom door closed. She heard the water stop running, heard him climb into the bath with a splash. He always overfilled the bath. If that water had overflowed, he could explain it to the grim Mrs White. Francesca hurriedly began to strip and then put on her dressing-gown. Thank heavens she had brought the warm one, which buttoned discreetly to her neck; a pretty blue robe made from fluffy angora wool.

Oliver re-emerged just as she was feeding the fire with fresh logs from the woven willow basket by the hearth. Her face flushed from the flames, her long hair plaited and dangling down her back, she glanced round and drew a sharp breath at the sight of him wandering across the room...totally naked.

She averted her eyes, got to her feet, gathered up her change of clothes from the bed, and darted towards the bathroom door.

'What's your hurry?' Oliver mocked, laughing.

Her teeth met. She slammed the bathroom door, and sank down on the side of the bath, fuming. If he was acting this way now, before dinner, what was he going to be like later, once she was in bed?

Oliver banged on the door. 'Don't take too long! I want my dinner!'

She ignored him and took as long as she chose; soaking luxuriously in the wonderful hot water. Mrs White had a rather Victorian taste in bath salts; she had a choice of either lavender or pine-scented ones. Francesca could smell the pine Oliver had picked. She chose lavender. It matched the demure little white blouse, the prim navy blue pleated skirt and the string of pearls she had decided to wear this evening.

Oliver contemplated her wryly before they went down to dinner. 'Now you look like a respectable married young lady,' he teased. 'Mrs White will be pleased!'

'I don't care what either you or Mrs White thinks!' Francesca made for the door. 'And, anyway, what was wrong with the way I was dressed before?'

'In those jeans and sweaters?' Oliver said softly, opening the door for her. 'Oh, no, you looked far too mysterious and sexy. Why, how did Mrs White know you were my wife? A blonde in tight jeans and a come-hither smile? You could have been my girlfriend!'

'No, I couldn't,' she snapped. 'I've got more sense.'

Mrs White saw them enter the bar and came to meet them. She showed them to a private dining-room where they ate alone together. There was no pretence of glamour; no candles on the table, no flowers or silver. The food was plain English cooking, but it was very good, and they were both hungry. They didn't miss the trappings of *cordon bleu* eating, and after the food they lingered over their cups of strong instant coffee. The snow had stopped falling outside; the lights of the public house gave the brilliance of a stained glass window to their reflections in the crystalline snow.

Oliver congratulated Mrs White again when she came to remove their coffee-cups; a polite reminder of the time. Francesca was stunned when she looked at the clock to see that it was only just past ten. It felt like the middle of the night. So much had happened that day. She had lost all sense of time.

She yawned. Mrs White said approvingly, 'Your wife is tired, she'll be wanting to get to bed.'

'Goodnight, thank you,' Francesca said, yawning again helplessly as she made for the stairs.

Oliver came up behind her; the old wooden stairs creaked under his weight. A deep-toned long-case clock chimed somewhere; a quarter past ten.

Francesca had left her nightdress on the bed; she picked it up and went to the bathroom to change again. She took her time, brushing her hair, cleansing her face, cleaning her teeth, then she opened the door into the bedroom and Oliver was carefully piling ash on to the fire to keep the warmth in all night. He got up as Francesca ran across the room in the long white Victorian-style gown, all frills and ruffles and lace.

She was disturbed by the way he looked at her; his eyes had a worrying gleam in them. She wasn't going to let him undermine her, though. She pretended not to notice.

'You can have the bathroom now,' she said distantly, not looking in his direction as she slid between the sheets. She expected them to be cold, but while she and Oliver were at dinner someone—Mrs White, presumably—had been up to put hot-water bottles in the bed and her wary toes found themselves reaching down into delicious warmth. She groaned with delight, 'Hot-water bottles!' and snuggled down, her heavy eyelids closing.

'What did you say?' Oliver asked, pausing on his way to the bathroom.

She yawned explosively. 'Hot-water bottles . . . in the bed . . . heavenly.'

'Well, you can hand them over,' said Oliver. 'You won't be needing them. You've got the bed, and I'll be freezing on the floor. Oh, and don't go to sleep just yet—I want two of those pillows and that velvet bedcover, too.'

'When you come back from the bathroom . . .' Francesca said, yawning again, and Oliver seemed to accept that because he vanished and she began to sink into a deep, consuming, blissful sleep. It was, she thought, like being swallowed by a vast marshmallow. The bed was so soft and warm and deliriously soothing, and she was very, very tired.

Some time during the night, she began to dream that she was in bed with Oliver, cuddled up to him, pressing her face into his chest, so close that she could hear the strong beat of his heart deep inside his ribcage. Francesca's lids fluttered, her lashes brushing against him. Her lips parted, her tonguetip licked his nipple, tasting the faint saltiness of his flesh, her hands stroked downwards over the taut flanks and flat belly until her palm felt the curl of wiry hair, and then Oliver groaned thickly, reaching for her, and Francesca woke up to find him naked in her arms, his body hard and insistent.

She gave a harsh, wordless cry of protest, then angrily said, 'What are you doing in my bed? You promised to sleep on the floor. I might have known I couldn't trust you.'

'I spent hours on that damn floor until the fire went out and I started getting cramp and aching all over from the draught under the door,' he said, his mouth sulky. 'And your bed looked so warm and comfortable, and it seemed big enough for six, let alone two. You were fast asleep, I didn't think you'd notice until morning, and by then it wouldn't matter anyway.' He looked at her through his lashes, a glitter in those grey eyes, his mouth curving in triumph. 'And I didn't make advances to you, darling. You made them to me, and very inviting you were, too...'

A burning flush crept up her face; she looked away, trembling. She had given herself away; she was betrayed and there was nobody to blame but herself. Oliver was not going to listen to any denials; breathing audibly, he began kissing her throat, his hands exploring everywhere, leaving a trail of fire across her flesh which all her cold common sense could not put out.

'Darling, you've driven me almost out of my mind. I want you badly—tell me you want me, tell me you love me,' he hoarsely whispered.

She felt his hands move and caress, his palms cupping her bared breasts, and her white flesh ached with rioting blood, her nipples hardened unbearably, but she wouldn't give him the admission he wanted. He might have won this battle, tonight, she knew her own stinging desire was too urgent to be denied this time; she could not go on fighting him, she wanted him too much, but only tonight, only now. There was always another day, and the war wasn't over yet.

His body slid over on top of her; he had pushed up her long, puritanical nightdress and she was naked from the neck down, naked and trembling helplessly as she yielded to him. His lips were hard and hot on hers with all the power of the conqueror; she resented it, his open triumph; and yet a bitter-sweet sensuality swept through her and she felt herself arching hungrily to meet the dominating thrust of his flesh. She stopped thinking and was clamouring and open, moist to receive the male in that primitive rite. Oliver entered her and she clasped his back with both hands as they rode on the bed; Francesca stifling her moans of pleasure on his bare shoulder, shuddering and biting him, past trying to hide from him the piercing ecstasy climbing inside her.

She had never felt such sensual intensity; they had always been good lovers, but their lovemaking had never been this passionate, and her wild cries almost deafened her to Oliver's gasping moans of satisfaction. Her heart was still beating like a sledgehammer when he collapsed on to her, his breathing ragged as he slowly recovered.

Francesca lay with his head on her breast, staring at the ceiling, filled with the usual sadness as her passion ebbed away, thinking of nothing. Suddenly her blue eyes opened wide as she was hit by a realisation.

Neither of them had used a contraceptive! It had all happened too quickly; the last thing she had intended was to sleep with Oliver tonight, and when she woke up to find him in her bed it had been too late.

Oliver sleepily kissed her bare shoulder, then raised his head to kiss her mouth. 'I love you, Fran,' he whispered.

She gave a little heave and he rolled off her, then sat up, leaning on his elbow to frown down at her.

'Fran, I need to get some sleep. I've hardly had any tonight. While you were snoring in this bed I was trying to get comfortable on that draughty floor, so can we talk about whatever is bugging you in the morning?'

'In the morning I am going to see a lawyer about this divorce.'

'There won't be a divorce,' Oliver said sharply.

'Do you really think that just because we had sex I'm going to forget that I saw you kissing Janice?'

'You saw Janice kissing me!'

Francesca gave him a contemptuous look. 'Oh, she forced herself on you, did she?'

'Yes, that's just what she did! I was just sitting behind my desk one minute, with Janice standing next to me, and the next second she had flung herself on my lap and was kissing me!' Oliver grated, scowling. 'I didn't know what the hell was happening until after you'd walked in . . . then you rushed out and I saw Janice's face and knew that she must have seen your shadow on the glass in the office door.'

'What?' Francesca stared fixedly at him, eyes widening.

'How long did you stand outside the door?' Oliver asked, and she thought back.

'I can't remember…half a minute, maybe. I paused to listen, in case you were talking on the phone, I think.'

'And Janice saw your shadow, and thought this was her chance to get her own back…'

'Get her own back?' repeated Francesca, watching him with an almost painful concentration.

'On me,' said Oliver, his mouth twisting.

'What had you done to her?'

'Fired her!'

Francesca was still trying to make up her mind whether or not to believe him. Oliver was clever and plausible; that was why he was such a brilliant salesman. What was he trying to sell her? How much truth was there in this story?

'Shrewd move,' she said sarcastically. 'But too late. You should have broken up with her weeks ago when I first came to London. I only had the vaguest suspicions then; you could easily have convinced me I was crazy, we could have got back together again then—now I know too much, Janice made sure of that. I hate the thought of a divorce, for Jon's sake, if not for our own, but I can't forgive you, Oliver, not after all these lies and betrayals. It's over…' She wanted to cry as she said it; it made her heart crack as if it was breaking inside her, she loved him and hated him because he had hurt her more than she could bear.

Oliver tried to put his arm around her. 'Fran, darling, don't,' he muttered unsteadily. 'You still love me, we just proved that…'

'We proved I still enjoy sex with you! I'd probably enjoy it just as much with some other attractive guy!'

Oliver breathed hoarsely. 'I don't believe that . . . you couldn't . . . I'd kill you if I thought . . .' He lay there in silence for a moment, then said flatly, 'I swear to you, I never had an affair with Janice.'

'Oh, please! No more lies!' she said furiously.

Oliver sat up in bed, still naked, his body taut, his face dark with anger.

'How can I prove it to you, for goodness' sake? It's all a question of whether or not you believe me, isn't it? And if you can't accept my word, after being my wife for ten years, you really don't think very much of me! I'd be wasting my time trying to convince you that although I liked Janice and we got on well, as far as working together went, I never had an affair with her. I've never slept with her or even really dated her, not in the personal sense.'

Francesca sat up, pulling her white nightdress down over her body, feeling more at ease at once, now that she was covered and hidden from him.

'What does that mean, for heaven's sake? How do you date someone—but not in the personal sense? Can you date someone impersonally? Or do you mean it was personal, but it wasn't a date?'

The sarcasm irritated him. He ran an impatient hand through his thick, black hair, smoothing it down where her urgent fingers had so recently ruffled and dishevelled it in the wildness of their lovemaking.

'It isn't easy to put into words——'

'I'll bet!' she interrupted bitingly, and he glared at her.

'Can you let me get a word out? Janice was my secretary, and a damn good one, too. I had to see a lot of her. It's unavoidable for a boss to see a lot of his secretary, in the office and out of it, but it was never personal; never just us two alone, certainly never with sex in mind, or romance, or whatever name you want to give it. It was always office business: dinner with clients, receptions, cocktail parties, trips abroad.'

'Oh, yes, those trips abroad... just you and Janice, staying in some hotel?'

'Once or twice, maybe, it was just the two of us, but no more than that. Usually there was a whole team of us, and anyway, I told you... there was never anything but business, Francesca! I never damned well slept with her.'

'Maybe you hadn't got that far,' Francesca said, looking into the angry grey eyes and feeling a queer little tremor run through her. He was very convincing, and she wanted to be convinced, but wasn't that just the danger? She was hoping he would convince her.

He had fired Janice, she was going, and Francesca knew that all his attention was focused back on herself, which was where she wanted it to be. Hadn't that been her plan in joining him in London? Oliver belonged to her. She had talked Matt into giving her a job so that she could be near Oliver every day. She had never meant to let him go without a fight, and Janice had known that, just as she had known that Janice wanted him, too, and would fight for him.

'I suppose you're going to tell me you didn't even know she fancied you?' she mocked, and Oliver shrugged.

'I knew she liked me. She made it pretty obvious, in fact she was rather too obvious about it. Men like to be the ones who do the hunting; they don't like to feel like they are being hunted. Janice chased me too hard; it was beginning to annoy me.'

'If it annoyed you, why did you keep her on?' Francesca said at once, her face unbelieving.

He gave her an ironic smile, his grey eyes gleaming between black lashes, like water hidden behind dark reeds. 'She was a good secretary, as I said. I was reluctant to have my working arrangements upset just because the stupid girl had designs on me...I could handle it well enough until you left me and she thought her big chance had come.'

Francesca frowned, suddenly sorry for Janice. Had she really loved Oliver? Or had it all been ambition and a desire for the status of his wife?

'What will she do now?' she asked flatly.

'I've fixed her a job with one of our clients in Tokyo. They were looking for an English executive, to handle English deals from their end. They wanted a man, but I talked them into taking Janice. I think she'll be quite pleased, once she has thought about it. If she works hard, she'll rise in that company. They reward merit, and Janice is clever and shrewd. I think she'll go a very long way.'

'As long as she stays there,' Francesca said.

'She's out of our lives,' Oliver promised.

'She'd better be.'

'Fran, I love you,' he said seriously, looking into her eyes.

'I'm not living at Lambourne any more.'

'We'll live in London during the week, and go back to Lambourne at weekends,' he promised.

'Except when Jon is home from school,' she told him. 'He will want to be at Lambourne for most of his holidays. But while I'm in London I want to go on working. I am not going to be bored out of my skull again. I want a job.'

'Well, I had an idea...' Oliver said. 'I wondered if you would like to take over Janice's job?'

She hadn't expected that, and bit her lip. 'I was thinking of running the advertising and publicity side, actually. You only have one girl doing it, and she isn't very good. I have ideas I'd like to try out. I don't just want to be a secretary all my life. I am a director and a major shareholder, remember!'

'You frighten me,' Oliver said, staring at her. 'How much control over my company am I going to have left in a few years' time, I wonder?'

'We started the company, didn't we? The three of us...you, me and Matt. You didn't mind sharing everything then. Why be so bothered about it now? And I did a good job with Mr Abbey, selling Porta to him, didn't I?'

'OK, OK, I give in,' Oliver groaned, taking her face between his hands and kissing her hard. 'Run whichever department you like! Do you want mine? I wouldn't dare try to stand in your way. But, darling, can we get to sleep? I can hardly keep my eyes open, and if we're going to take Jon out tomorrow we are going to need all the energy we've got.'

She kissed him back and cuddled close to him, his arms around her again, his chin pillowed on her head. She had got him back and she was never going to let him drift away from her again. She mustn't be greedy, of course; she had been given so much when she was afraid she had lost everything; but there was just one more thing she longed for . . . and tonight she felt somehow that it might actually happen. This was such a special night, with the snow blowing outside and the passion and warmth flowering in this room. A magic night, on which a baby might be conceived . . . Francesca held on to her man and prayed for one more miracle.

Coming Next Month

Available in September wherever paperback books are sold, or through Harlequin Reader Service:

In the U.S.
901 Fuhrmann Blvd.
P.O. Box 1397
Buffalo, N.Y. 14240-1397

In Canada
P.O. Box 603
Fort Erie, Ontario
L2A 5X3

HARLEQUIN
American Romance™

THE LOVES OF A CENTURY...

Join American Romance in a nostalgic look back at the Twentieth Century—at the lives and loves of American men and women from the turn-of-the-century to the dawn of the year 2000.

Journey through the decades from the dance halls of the 1900s to the discos of the seventies ... from Glenn Miller to the Beatles ... from Valentino to Newman ... from corset to miniskirt ... from beau to Significant Other.

Relive the moments ... recapture the memories.

Look now for the CENTURY OF AMERICAN ROMANCE series in Harlequin American Romance. In one of the four American Romance titles appearing each month, for the next twelve months, we'll take you back to a decade of the Twentieth Century, where you'll relive the years and rekindle the romance of days gone by.

Don't miss a day of the CENTURY OF AMERICAN ROMANCE.

A CENTURY OF
AMERICAN ROMANCE
1900's

The women...the men...the passions...
the memories....

CAR-1

HARLEQUIN'S WISHBOOK
SWEEPSTAKES RULES & REGULATIONS
NO PURCHASE NECESSARY TO ENTER OR RECEIVE A PRIZE